# The Amazing Earth Model Book

## Easy-to-Make, Hands-on Models That Teach

by Donald M. Silver
and Patricia J. Wynne

SCHOLASTIC
**PROFESSIONAL BOOKS**

New York ◉ Toronto ◉ London ◉ Auckland ◉ Sydney

### Dedication

This book is dedicated to my friends
Marcella Corcoran, Yetta Levine, and Nina Albright

—D. M. S.

To L. D. H. on the lone prairie

—P. J. W.

### Acknowledgments

Thanks to Deborah Schecter and Mary Kay Carson for their excellent comments and suggestions and for the additional hands-on activities they contributed to this book.

Special thanks to David Silver for giving up vacation time when he was needed.

Edited by Mary Kay Carson

Cover design by Jaime Lucero and Vincent Ceci

Cover photo by Donnelly Marks

Interior design by Ellen Matlach Hassell
for Boultinghouse & Boultinghouse, Inc.

Interior illustrations by Patricia J. Wynne

ISBN: 0-590-93089-3

# Contents

# INTRODUCTION

Grow a
Volcano

Inside a Cave

**T**eaching earth science is literally teaching how the world works. Earth science includes the everyday natural world of rocks, minerals, rain, and erosion as well as extraordinary phenomena like volcanoes, earthquakes, and geysers. In *The Amazing Earth Model Book*, students will learn many key earth science concepts in a unique way— by building models that illustrate the workings of our planet.

Fossil
Timeline

Rock Field Guide

A River's Run

# Why Use Models to Teach Earth Science?

Using models to teach earth science is natural because models lend themselves to illustrating processes and spatial relationships—both key to understanding how our planet works. Earth isn't flat—it's three-dimensional, and it continually changes through geologic processes. Models can illustrate many processes and internal features of Earth better than text alone or two-dimensional drawings. By assembling and working with the models in this book, students will gain a sense of how volcanoes look from the inside out and what happens underground to produce a geyser.

Teaching with models also makes the learning process appealing to a more diverse group of learners. Tactile learners will excel at building the models while internalizing the concepts. Students who have difficulty visualizing spatial ideas will benefit from having a three-dimensional model they can see and handle. Constructing and coloring models is also a great way to fit art into your class curriculum.

The models and accompanying lessons and hands-on investigations featured in this book meet many of the National Science Education Standards, the set of criteria intended to guide the quality of science teaching and learning in this country. The standards outline key science content areas and support a hands-on, inquiry-based approach to learning. The chart below shows how the topics in this book correlate with the National Science Education Content Standards for grades K through 8.

## National Science Education Content Standards for Earth Science

### GRADES K–4

- Identifying and characterizing properties of earth materials including rocks, soils, and water.
- Understanding that soils have properties of color and texture and have the capacity to hold water.
- Inferring the nature of past plant and animal life through fossil evidence.
- Understanding that Earth's surface changes due to the processes of weathering, erosion, volcanoes, and earthquakes.

### GRADES 5–8

- Identifying and characterizing the three layers of the earth.
- Inferring that major geologic events such as earthquakes, volcanic eruptions, and mountain building result from the movement of crustal plates.
- Identifying the constructive and destructive forces that form land, such as volcanoes, weathering, erosion, and sedimentation.
- Understanding the rock cycle and how it results from plate movement and drives rock formation.
- Identifying the components of soil and the characteristics of soil layers.
- Understanding the water cycle and the solvent power of water.
- Inferring past conditions of Earth and its past plant and animal life through fossil evidence.

# What's Inside

Each of the six chapters in this book features a number of models related to that chapter's topic. Each individual model has a number of easy-to-identify features and sections, including:

### Model Illustration
This picture near the model's name gives you an idea of how the finished product looks. Its caption describes what the model illustrates.

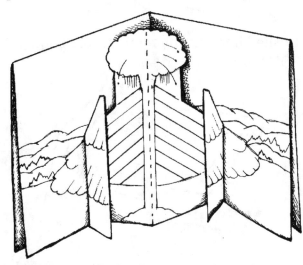

### Science Concepts & Objectives
The learning concepts and objectives to be achieved by the model and accompanying lesson.

### Vocabulary
Simple lesson-related definitions of key words. Note that vocabulary words aren't repeated within a chapter. For example, *earthquake* is defined under the first earthquake model in the Earthquakes chapter on page 100 and isn't repeated under successive earthquake models.

### For Your Information
A concise summary of the basic earth science background information needed to teach the lesson.

### Teaching With the Model
A lesson map for introducing the concepts to be conveyed for the particular model and step-by-step suggestions for teaching with it. Sidebars that provide additional information are also included for some models.

### Making the Model
Easy-to-follow assembly instructions with numerous diagrams and illustrations that simplify building each model. These can be photocopied and distributed to students who are making their own models.

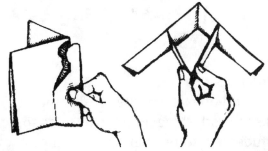

### Extensions
Related experiments and activities to extend learning.

**HANDS-ON** A hands-on experiment or activity that demonstrates one of the model's science concepts.

**COOPERATE AND CREATE** A cooperative-learning activity that challenges student groups to further explore that model's topic.

**RESEARCH IT** Suggested topics for independent research reports or projects that will spark students' interest.

## Reproducible Pages
Patterns for each model to be photocopied, cut out, and fashioned into the models.

## Resources
At the end of each chapter is a listing of books and other media related to the topic for students and teachers. A compilation of these resources, arranged by topic, begins on page 125.

# Helpful Model-Making Hints

◈ The thickest black lines on the reproducible pages are CUT lines.

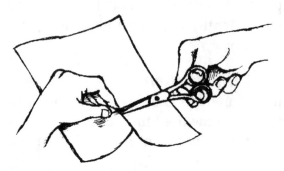

◈ Dashed lines on the reproducible pages are FOLD lines.

◈ Glue and tape can be used interchangeably to assemble the models.

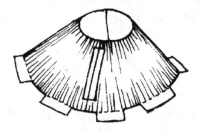

◈ If students will be coloring the models and using tape, have them color first so they won't have to color over the tape.

# Getting the Most Out of This Book

A quick look at the table of contents on page 3 will tell you about the topics covered in this book. The six chapters stand on their own and can be used in any order. Likewise, each individual model is complete within itself and can be used out of sequence or alone—feel free to pick and choose.

Here are some other useful tips for getting the most out of this book:

- Within a chapter, scanning the **Science Concepts & Objectives** for each model will help you to find the appropriate model to illustrate the concept you would like to teach.

- Make and use the models to best fit your class's earth science curriculum needs. You might prefer to make some models yourself to use in a class demonstration or to display in discovery centers, while students would benefit from making other models themselves.

- It's a good idea always to make any model yourself first before using it as a class project. That way you can assess its complexity and appropriateness for your class. Not only will this save you time if you decide to have the entire class make the model, but you will also likely discover ways to make the best use of each model in teaching your curriculum. Your finished model can serve as a guide for students to study as they make their own models.

- Consider using individual models outside of your science lessons. For example, make the cave model when reading *The Adventures of Tom Sawyer* or build one of the volcano models to accompany reading a recent volcano news story.

Feel free to adapt, change, and use the models, experiments, and activities in this book to suit the unique needs of your students. You know best how to excite and maintain your class's interest in how Earth works. Enjoy!

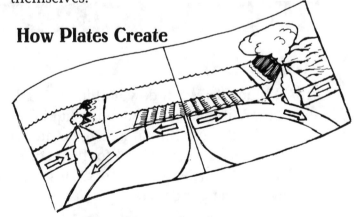

**How Plates Create**

**Make a Mountain**

**Weathering Park**

# Earth's Layers

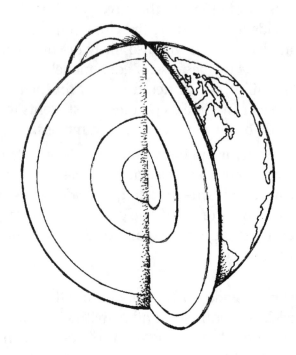

## Inside Earth

This model shows Earth's layers—the crust, mantle, outer core, and inner core.

### SCIENCE CONCEPTS & OBJECTIVES

- Identify Earth's layers and their characteristics
- Infer that liquid rock from the mantle can rise up through the crust

### VOCABULARY

**core** Earth's super-hot center—the outer core is liquid and the inner core solid

**crust** Earth's cool outer layer of mostly solid rock

**mantle** Earth's vast middle layer

## For Your Information

You'd have to travel about 4,000 miles (6,400 kilometers) down to reach Earth's center. On the way you'd pass through hard *crust,* hot mushy *mantle,* super-hot liquid *outer core,* and dense solid *inner core.*

These churning layers beneath the crust make our planet geologically active. And where the crust is thin, weak, or cracked, liquid rock rising up from the mantle can create a volcano.

## TEACHING WITH THE MODEL

## Inside Earth

1. Ask students: What do you think is inside Earth? Is it hot or cold? Solid or liquid? How far do you think it is to the center of Earth? As far as from here to the moon? From Los Angeles to New York? Has anyone ever gone there?

2. Invite students to make the model (see page 11) and then color the four layers.

3. Point out each layer and discuss its characteristics (see Inside Our Earth, page 12). Challenge students to write down each layer's thickness and one other fact about that layer on their model.

# Making the Model

## Inside Earth

**MATERIALS:** reproducible pages 13 and 14 ⊙ scissors ⊙ glue or tape ⊙ crayons, colored pencils, or markers

1. Photocopy pages 13 and 14.

2. Cut out the four circles. Fold each circle in half along the dashed line with the printed side facing in.

3. Place the circle with the map facedown. Dot glue or press rolls of tape on the left side of the circle.

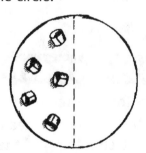

4. Place the folded circle labeled CRUST faceup on top of the taped half of the map circle so the circle edges match exactly.

5. With the CRUST circle folded closed, tape as shown.

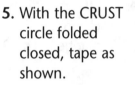

6. Repeat steps 4 and 5 using the circle labeled MANTLE. Dot glue or press rolls of tape on the left side of the CRUST circle. Then glue or tape the folded MANTLE circle to the back of the folded CRUST circle.

7. Repeat steps 4 and 5 using the circle labeled OUTER CORE and INNER CORE. Tape it to the back of the folded MANTLE circle.

8. Tape or glue the other half of the CORE circle to the map circle.

4. Invite students to add up the thicknesses and then ask: How far is it to Earth's center? *(Earth is about 4,000 miles or 6,400 kilometers thick from crust to center. That's about the distance from Chicago to London, England.)*

5. Ask: In what layer is there hot liquid rock? *(mantle)* Point out that liquid, molten rock can rise up and break through weak or cracked crust under land and water. What does that cause? *(a volcano)*

# Inside Our Earth

⟐ The *crust* is Earth's outer layer. It's mostly rock. Under the continents, the crust is up to 25 miles (40 kilometers) thick. Under the ocean, it is about 3 to 6 miles (5 to 10 kilometers) thick. If you compared Earth to an apple, the crust would almost be as thin as the apple's skin. Though no one has yet drilled to the bottom of the crust, the deeper people dig, the hotter it gets.

⟐ The *mantle* is Earth's middle layer. It is very hot and under a lot of pressure. Scientists think that the top and bottom parts of the mantle are rigid rock. But in between are rocks so hot that they flow like a thick syrup. The mantle is 1,789 miles (2,880 kilometers) thick.

⟐ The *outer* and *inner cores* are together larger than Mars. The outer core is 1,410 miles (2,270 kilometers) thick. The inner core is 756 miles (1,216 kilometers) thick. The core is the hottest part of Earth. In fact, the inner core temperature may reach 7,200°F (4,000°C). Scientists think that the outer core is a hot liquid rich in iron and nickel. The movement of this liquid is believed to cause Earth's magnetic field. The inner core is mostly solid iron and nickel.

## EXTENSIONS

### HANDS-ON
# 3-D Earth Model

**Students create a three-dimensional model of Earth to better understand its layered composition.**

**MATERIALS:** at least four different colors of clay ⊙ butter knife

1. Invite students to roll a piece of clay into a ball. This represents Earth's inner core.

2. Next ask students to completely cover their balls with a layer of different-colored clay. This represents the outer core. Students repeat this step with another color of clay for the mantle. Have students use the model to estimate each layer's thickness.

3. A final covering represents the crust. It needs to be thin, so suggest that students pat the clay into a thin pancake before wrapping it around the ball.

4. To reveal the layers, invite students either to cut their Earths in half or cut out a quarter. They can make tags labeling each layer.

### COOPERATE AND CREATE
# Fact-filled Layers

Challenge students to find out more about Earth's layers. Draw a large diagram of Earth's layers on butcher paper and hang it on a wall or bulletin board. Divide students into four groups and assign each a layer. Have each group fill in their layer with facts and figures, as well as scientists' theories, about that layer of Earth.

## RESEARCH IT

Related topics for research reports or projects:

⟐ How deep have people drilled into Earth's crust? What technology did they use? What stopped them from going farther?

⟐ How does a compass work? What does it have to do with Earth's layers?

⟐ Earth is a geologically active planet, whereas our moon is geologically inactive. Are all planets geologically active? Are all moons inactive?

CRUST

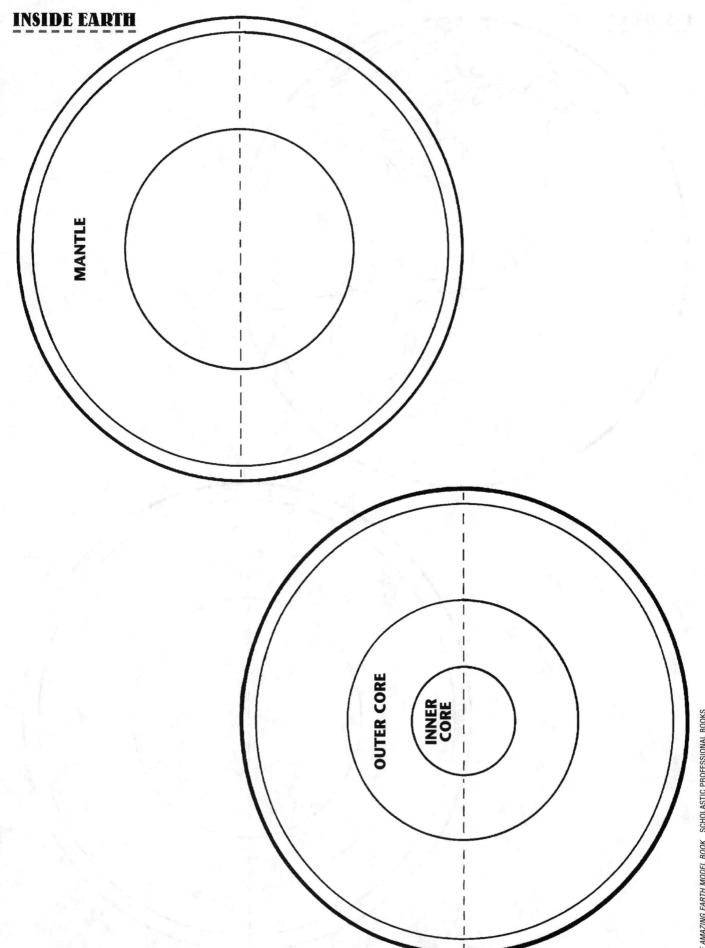

MANTLE

OUTER CORE

INNER CORE

THE AMAZING EARTH MODEL BOOK   SCHOLASTIC PROFESSIONAL BOOKS

# Volcano!

## Grow a Volcano

This model demonstrates how a volcano can grow into a mountain.

### SCIENCE CONCEPTS & OBJECTIVES

- ● Observe how volcanoes can grow into mountains
- ● Identify what comes out of a volcano
- ● Infer that a volcano can erupt anywhere

### VOCABULARY

**cone** a hill or mountain of ash and hardened lava built around a volcano's opening

**lava** melted rock that flows from a volcano

**volcano** an opening in Earth's crust where magma can escape

## For Your Information

A volcano erupts when molten rock and gases—called *magma*—spew through a crack in Earth's crust. This mostly happens where Earth's moving plates open up cracks and weak spots in the crust. But volcanoes can form anywhere there's a break in the crust, and there's no known way to prevent them.

When a volcano erupts, the gases escape into the air, and the liquid rock—now called *lava*—pours out. Spewed lava, cinders, and ash build up in layers around a volcano's opening and form a *cone*. These cones can grow into mountains over time.

## TEACHING WITH THE MODEL

## Grow a Volcano

1. Ask students: What is a volcano? What comes out of it? Has a volcano ever erupted near where you live? Could it? What would happen if one did?

2. Assemble the model's parts (see page 16).

3. Build the volcano (or have students build theirs) as you read the true story, Birth of a Volcano (reproducible page 18), to the class. Cues next to the story tell students when to add another cone on top and when to insert the fiery shower of lava plume. The volcano will appear to "grow" with the story as it keeps erupting and spewing out lava.

4. Following the story, check comprehension by reviewing the questions in step 1.

## Grow a Volcano

**MATERIALS:** reproducible pages 19 and 20 ⊙ scissors ⊙ ruler ⊙ tape ⊙ crayons, colored pencils, or markers (optional)

1. Photocopy pages 19 and 20.

2. Cut out the four pieces. Color them, if desired.

3. Cut the ends of the square piece, the LAVA PLUME, along the heavy black lines. Curl the paper strips by pulling each tightly over the edge of a ruler or the blade of blunt scissors.

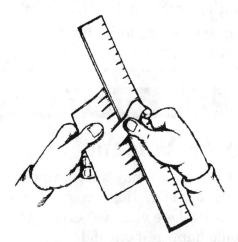

4. Next, roll the LAVA PLUME into a cylinder with the curled strips facing out. Wrapping it around a pencil, as shown, helps. Set it aside.

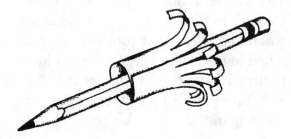

5. Tape each of the other three pieces into a cone, as shown.

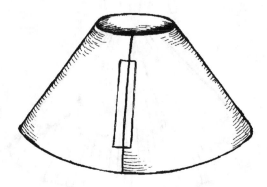

6. To model a growing volcano, stack the three cones one on top of the other and then insert the plume into the hole at the top.

## HANDS-ON

# Lumps of Lava

**Students discover how the thickness of a liquid affects the shape it makes.**

The shape a volcano takes is in part determined by how thick the lava is. Students can discover this for themselves by building volcano mountains out of runny and thick flour paste.

MATERIALS: flour ❂ water ❂ bowls ❂ spoons ❂ plates

1. Make two separate pastes by mixing flour and water in bowls. Make one the consistency of gravy and the other as thick as possible without becoming dough.

2. Invite students to build mountains by dripping spoonfuls of each paste onto two separate plates. Which "lava" makes a gently sloping shield cone volcano? *(runny paste)* Which makes a steeper cinder volcano? *(thick paste)* Which kind of volcano is Paricutin? *(steeper cinder cone volcano)*

## HANDS-ON

# Magma on the Move

**Students observe how magma under pressure pushes out of the ground through volcanoes.**

Hot magma under Earth's surface is under pressure. Sometimes it pushes up from underground through a volcano, changing Earth's surface. This demonstration simulates this process.

MATERIALS: tube of toothpaste, half full ❂ pin

1. Place the tube of toothpaste (with the cap on) on a desk. Ask students to imagine that the tube is the surface of Earth. The toothpaste inside is the hot, melted magma underground.

2. Distribute the toothpaste evenly in the tube. Then use the pin to make a tiny hole near the bottom. Ask students what the hole might represent. *(a volcano's opening)*

3. Press down on the tube near the cap. Ask students what this action might represent. *(magma under pressure)* What happens? *(The magma oozes out of the volcano.)*

## COOPERATE AND CREATE

# Classify Volcanoes

**Students work in groups to investigate the different kinds of land-forming volcanoes.**

Challenge student groups to research and make a poster of one of the three different kinds of land-forming volcanoes: cinder cone volcano, shield volcano, and composite volcano (a mixture of cinder cone and shield). Invite them to draw diagrams on their posters showing the volcano's characteristics as well as feature famous volcanoes that belong to their category.

## RESEARCH IT

Related topics for research reports or projects:

➥ How was the birth of the island volcano Surtsey off Iceland's coast in 1963 similar to the birth of Paricutin? How was it different?

➥ Not all volcanoes erupt and fall back asleep. The volcano Stromboli has been spitting out lava about every 20 minutes for hundreds of years. Why?

➥ The word *volcano* comes from the Roman god Vulcan. Why?

# Birth of a Volcano

One day in 1943, a Mexican farmer heard a loud rumble. He felt the earth shake and saw a large crack open in the ground. As smoke and hot gas spewed from the crack, the scared farmer ran to alert everyone in his village of danger.

That night, red-hot glowing rocks shot out of the crack. So did hot powdery ash. They piled up around the crack, forming a cone-shaped mound. **(1)**

The mound grew and grew. By the next afternoon, the cone was as high as a 12-story building. **(2)**

A volcano was born.

For weeks, hot rocks, ash, and gases kept shooting out of the growing volcano named Paricutin (pah-REE-coo-TEEN). Many trees caught fire, and layers of ash covered nearby homes and fields. One day, fiery hot lava started pouring out of the volcano. The lava destroyed everything in its path and buried the farmer's village a mile away. As the lava cooled, it hardened into solid rock. By the end of the year, Paricutin stood almost 1,000 feet (300 meters) high. **(3)**

A river of lava flowed out of the volcano, burying a town five miles (eight kilometers) away. While all the villagers fled to safety, only the church bell towers stood unharmed above the lava. After nine years, Paricutin stopped rumbling. **(4)**

No one knows if it will ever erupt again.

## MODEL CUES

1. Set down the smallest cone of ash and insert the lava plume.

2. Remove the lava plume. Top the small cone with the midsized cone of ash and reinsert the lava plume.

3. Remove the lava plume. Add the final large cone of lava and ash to the stack and reinsert the lava plume.

4. Remove the lava plume.

THE AMAZING EARTH MODEL BOOK   SCHOLASTIC PROFESSIONAL BOOKS

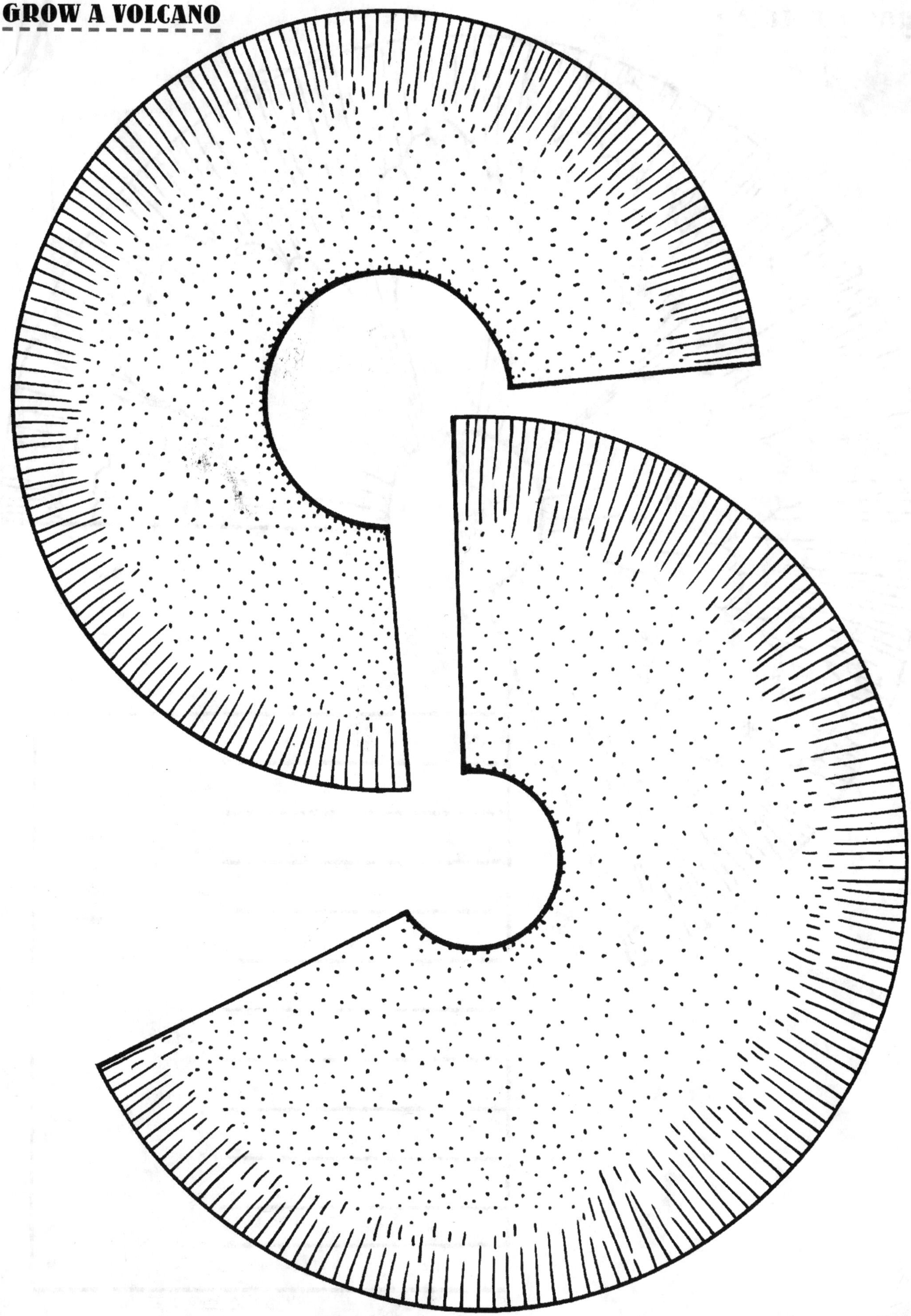

THE AMAZING EARTH MODEL BOOK   SCHOLASTIC PROFESSIONAL BOOKS

# Volcano Anatomy

## Inside a Volcano

This model shows the parts of an erupting volcano.

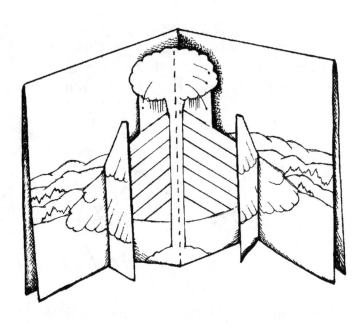

### SCIENCE CONCEPTS & OBJECTIVES

◈ Identify the path magma takes as it rises inside a volcano, loses its gases, and becomes lava

◈ Infer the potential destructiveness of an erupting volcano's intense heat, deadly gases, fiery lava, and explosive power

### VOCABULARY

**magma** underground molten rock and gases from the mantle

**volcanic bombs** falling lava that has cooled into large balls

## For Your Information

Lava starts out inside Earth's mantle as *magma*—hot syrupy liquid rock and gases. When magma rises and breaks through a crack or weak spot in the crust, a volcano is created. High pressure keeps the gases dissolved in the magma while underground. But as magma reaches the surface, the gases separate from the liquid rock.

If the gases separate slowly, a volcano gently erupts. The gases simply escape into the air as the molten rock—now called *lava*—oozes out. The lava that flows down the sides of the mountain cools and hardens into rock. However, if the gases are very hot and under very high pressure, they grow into larger and larger bubbles underground and explode violently at the surface. When a volcano

explodes like this, lava shoots up into the air like a fountain of fire. As that lava falls and cools, it becomes powdery ash, stone chunks, or bowling ball–sized *volcanic bombs*.

## TEACHING WITH THE MODEL

## Inside a Volcano

1. Ask students: What makes a volcano like Paricutin erupt? Why does lava flow out of volcanoes? Where does it come from?

2. Invite students to make the model (see page 22).

*(continued on page 23)*

# Making the Model ✂

## Inside a Volcano

**MATERIALS:** reproducible page 25 and bottom of page 30 ◉ scissors ◉ tape ◉ crayons, colored pencils, or markers (optional)

1. Photocopy page 25 and the bottom of page 30 labeled FLAP PIECE. Color all the pieces, if desired.

2. On page 25, cut along the thick black line. This frees the top half of the volcano from the page but leaves the bottom half intact.

3. Fold page 25 in half along the horizontal dashed line so the printed side is on the outside.

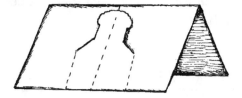

4. Fold the page in half again along the dashed line so the volcano is inside.

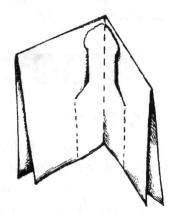

5. Now fold the model back in the opposite direction so the volcano is on the outside. Firmly crease the fold along the volcano.

6. Pinch the volcano along its fold. While holding the volcano, open up the model and refold to close it with the volcano inside. Firmly crease both the new and old folds.

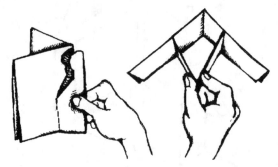

7. Cut out the FLAP PIECE on page 30. Tape the FLAP PIECE onto the volcano's vertical dashed lines. The bottom of the FLAP PIECE should be even with the bottom of the folded volcano.

8. Cut open the FLAP PIECE along the middle thick black line. Fold the model closed so the cover with the title is on top. When the model is opened, it should work like a "pop-up."

*(continued from page 21)*

3. Point out the lava flowing down the outside of the erupting volcano's cone. Ask: Where did it come from?

4. Have students open the cone to find out. *(The lava rose from the magma chamber up through the vent.)* Ask: What is magma? Invite students to label the magma chamber "Melted rock and gases."

5. Have students locate the cloud of gas, steam, and ash above the volcano's opening. Ask: Where did the gases come from? *(magma)*

6. Ask students to find the ash and bombs. Ask: How were they formed? *(by falling and cooling lava that was shot in the air)*

7. Have students open the cones again and find the slanted layers of hardened lava and ash. Ask: How did they get there? *(past eruptions)* Which are the oldest? *(ones closest to the vent)*

8. Challenge students to draw side vents branching off from the main vent channel, as shown.

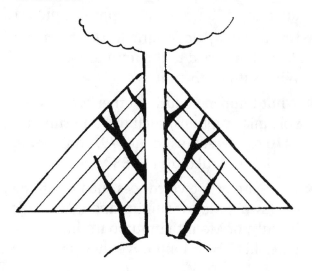

## HANDS-ON
# Shake a Soda

**Students observe what happens when a gaseous liquid under pressure is released.**

MATERIALS: 2 plastic screw-cap bottles, one filled with club soda, one filled with tap water ◉ dishpan or sink ◉ paper towels

1. Open both bottles. Ask: What happens? *(Gas bubbles fizz to the surface in the soda bottle where they burst and escape into the air. No gas appears in the water bottle.)* Ask: Where did the soda's gas come from? *(It was dissolved in the soda at the factory and trapped there under pressure of the closed bottle.)*

2. Recap the bottles and shake them. Ask students to predict: What will happen when each bottle is opened?

3. Sit the bottles in a dishpan and open them. Be careful to hold each bottle firmly and pointed away from you or students. Ask: What happened? *(The soda's gas rose fast and foamed out of the top pushing soda along with it.)* How is this like what happens when a volcano explodes? *(Gas bubbles in magma are released as they leave the volcano and push the molten rock with it.)*

## HANDS-ON
# Cooling Volcanoes

**Students investigate how blocking sunlight affects temperature.**

This activity demonstrates how some volcanoes spew tons of ash and gases into the air that can block sunlight for days and cause lower temperatures.

**MATERIALS:** 2 plastic report covers, one clear and one colored ◉ white paper ◉ 2 thermometers

1. Fold each report cover in half so it's like a tent.

2. When the sun is directly overhead, set two sheets of paper on a sunny windowsill. Set one of the tented folders on each sheet of paper and place a thermometer in the tent.

3. After 20 minutes, check the temperatures and record them. Ask: Which got hotter? Why? *(The thermometer under the clear report cover got hotter because it received more direct sunlight. The colored cover blocked some sun.)* How is this like what happens with large volcanic eruptions? *(Ash and gases expelled into the atmosphere by the volcano block out sunlight, and temperatures drop.)*

## COOPERATE AND CREATE
# Mount St. Helens

**Student groups make filmstrips of the eruption of a famous volcano.**

Tell students how, in 1980, Mount St. Helens in Washington State erupted, blowing off an entire face of the mountain.

**MATERIALS:** reproducible page 26 ◉ scissors ◉ tape ◉ pint milk cartons ◉ crayons

1. Copy and hand out page 26. Ask students to read the story and cut out the six pictures. If they like, students can color them.

2. Challenge students to put the pictures in chronological order. Ask them to label the ordered pictures from 1 to 6 in the small upper left-hand boxes. Then have students tape the ordered pictures together to make a filmstrip.

3. Next make viewers from pint milk cartons. Cut off both ends of the carton to make a tube. About an inch from one end of the tube, cut slits on two opposite sides of the carton. The slits should run the length of the sides and allow for easy passage of the filmstrip.

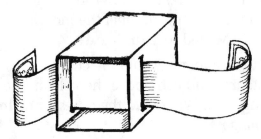

4. Invite students to view their filmstrips. Thread a filmstrip through the viewer and hold it up to a light or window as you pull the strip through, picture by picture. Challenge student groups to write a frame-by-frame script to accompany their filmstrip, using the story for help.

## RESEARCH IT

Related topics for research reports or projects:

◆ For how long did Mount St. Helens erupt? What happened to the land around it? What's it like there now?

◆ What happened during other famous volcanic eruptions, such as Santorini in 1470 B.C., Vesuvius in A.D. 79, Tambora in 1815, and Krakatau in 1883?

◆ What are active volcanoes such as Kilauea in Hawaii, Mount Fuji in Japan, Mount Etna in Italy, or Mount Pinatubo in the Philippines like? How long have they been active?

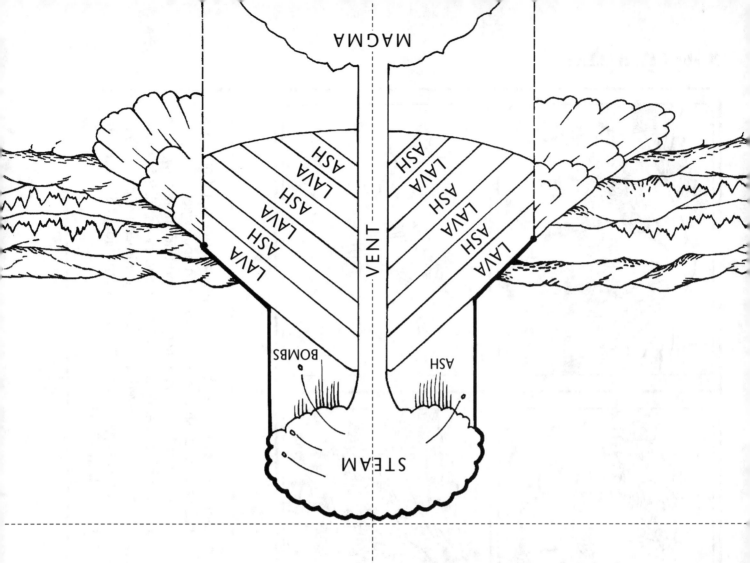

MAGMA

ASH
LAVA
ASH
LAVA
ASH
LAVA
ASH
LAVA

VENT

BOMBS
ASH

STEAM

# Inside a Volcano

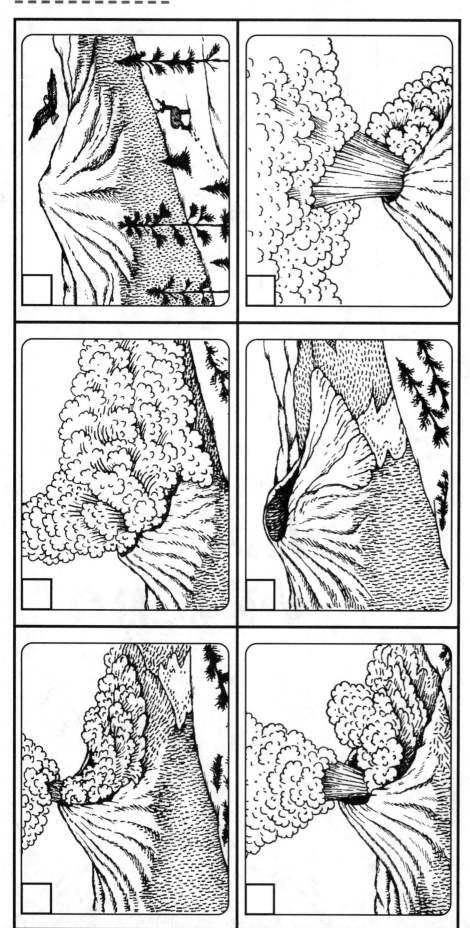

# A Volcano Explodes

It is Sunday morning, May 18, 1980. All is quiet around Mount St. Helens in Washington State. An eagle soars high in the sky. Deer nibble on leaves in a nearby forest. Suddenly the ground begins to shake. There is a tremendous explosion with more power than hundreds of atomic bombs. The top of the mountain is blown to bits. In seconds, a black cloud of very hot gases and ash covers the mountain and sweeps down over miles of forest. Soon fiery lava and thick mud flow down the mountainside. By the time the cloud clears, all is in ruins. The forest is destroyed. Thousands of animals are dead. So are about 50 people. After 123 years asleep, Mount St. Helens has woken with a fury!

*THE AMAZING EARTH MODEL BOOK*   SCHOLASTIC PROFESSIONAL BOOKS

# Volcano Craters

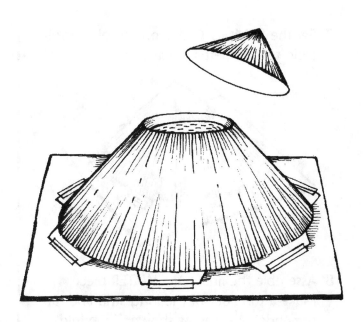

## Create a Crater

This model shows how volcanoes form craters.

### SCIENCE CONCEPTS & OBJECTIVES

- Identify different ways that craters form on volcanoes
- Review how a volcano works

### VOCABULARY

**crater** bowl-shaped pit at the top of a volcano

## For Your Information

Most volcanoes have a crater at the top. A very explosive volcano can form a crater by simply blasting off its top, leaving a crater behind. Craters can also be formed after an eruption stops and lava sinks back down into the vent. Sometimes the entire volcano's summit collapses inward. This happens when most of the magma inside a volcano pours out or drains back down inside Earth's crust. Without the magma for support, the summit collapses into an enormous crater. Some craters are miles across and nearly a mile deep. If the crater fills with rain or melted snow, it can turn into a crater lake.

## TEACHING WITH THE MODEL

## Create a Crater

1. Ask students: What would be left if the top of a volcanic mountain blew itself apart during an explosive eruption? *(a crater)* What do you think would happen if the top of a volcano collapsed after an eruption was over? *(a crater)*

2. Assemble the model's four parts (see pages 30 and 31). Put the small SUMMIT CONE on top of the volcano and set the LAKE WATER aside for now.

3. Ask: How does a volcano work? Let students review the process.

*(continued on page 29)*

# Making the Model

## Create a Crater

**MATERIALS:** reproducible pages 30 and 31 ⊙ crayons, colored pencils, or markers (optional) ⊙ scissors ⊙ tape ⊙ cardboard or stiff paper

1. Photocopy pages 30 and 31. Color the pieces, if desired.

2. Cut out the four pieces.

3. Tape together the edges of the two large identical pieces, as shown.

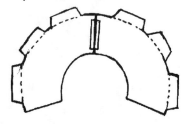

4. Then tape the other ends of the pieces together. The taped pieces should form the bottom half of a cone, as shown.

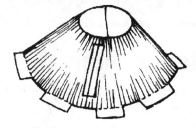

5. Fold out the flaps along the volcano's base. Then set the volcano on a piece of cardboard or stiff paper and tape each tab to the cardboard.

6. Tape the small C-shaped piece together to form a small SUMMIT CONE.

7. Set the SUMMIT CONE on top of the volcano to complete its peak.

8. Assemble the final LAKE WATER piece. Make a tube out of the long strip and tape the ends together, as shown. Then fold down the LAKE WATER lid's flap and fold the tab into the tube. Tape the tab from inside the tube.

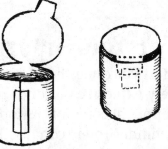

9. When placing the LAKE WATER tube into the crater, be sure the water side is up.

*(continued from page 27)*

4. Invite students to make their summits explode by flicking off the SUMMIT CONE. Ask: What's left? *(a crater)* Ask: What would happen if the crater filled with rain or melted snow? *(A lake would form.)* Have students insert the cutout LAKE WATER into the cylinder to create a crater lake or fit a small paper cup into the cylinder and fill it with water.

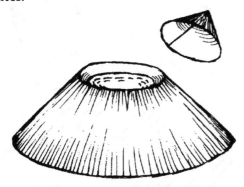

## EXTENSIONS

### HANDS-ON
# Tumbling Tops

**Students discover how liquid can support structures, like magma supports the summit of a volcano.**

MATERIALS: gallon-sized plastic bag ⊙ twist tie ⊙ 2-quart cooking pot ⊙ dishpan or sink ⊙ paper clip or pushpin

1. Fill the plastic bag completely with water and close it tightly. Place the pot in the dishpan or sink. Then set the bag inside the pot with one bottom corner of the bag sticking up, like a mountain. Now top off that corner with the small SUMMIT CONE piece from the model.

2. Ask: What's holding the cone up? *(water)* Predict: What would happen if the water was gone? Pierce the bag near its base with the pushpin or paper clip and observe what happens. Ask: How is this like what happens when a volcano's summit collapses and forms a crater? *(When a volcano erupts and most of the magma flows out, the rocks above the magma can collapse.)*

## COOPERATE AND CREATE
# Create Clay Craters

**Student groups model the crater-creating process by making a series of clay volcanoes.**

Challenge student groups to make a series of three to five clay models of a volcano as it erupts and a crater is formed. The Mount St. Helen's filmstrip on page 26 provides one example to follow. However, encourage students to find other "before and after" photos of Mt. Pinatubo or other recent eruptions to use as models. Each volcano stage should be accompanied by an information card that explains what's happening.

## RESEARCH IT

Related topics for research reports or projects:

❧ Crater Lake in Oregon is the deepest lake in the United States—and it's a volcanic crater. When was the last time its volcano erupted?

❧ How are craters on the moon or meteor craters on Earth different from volcanic craters?

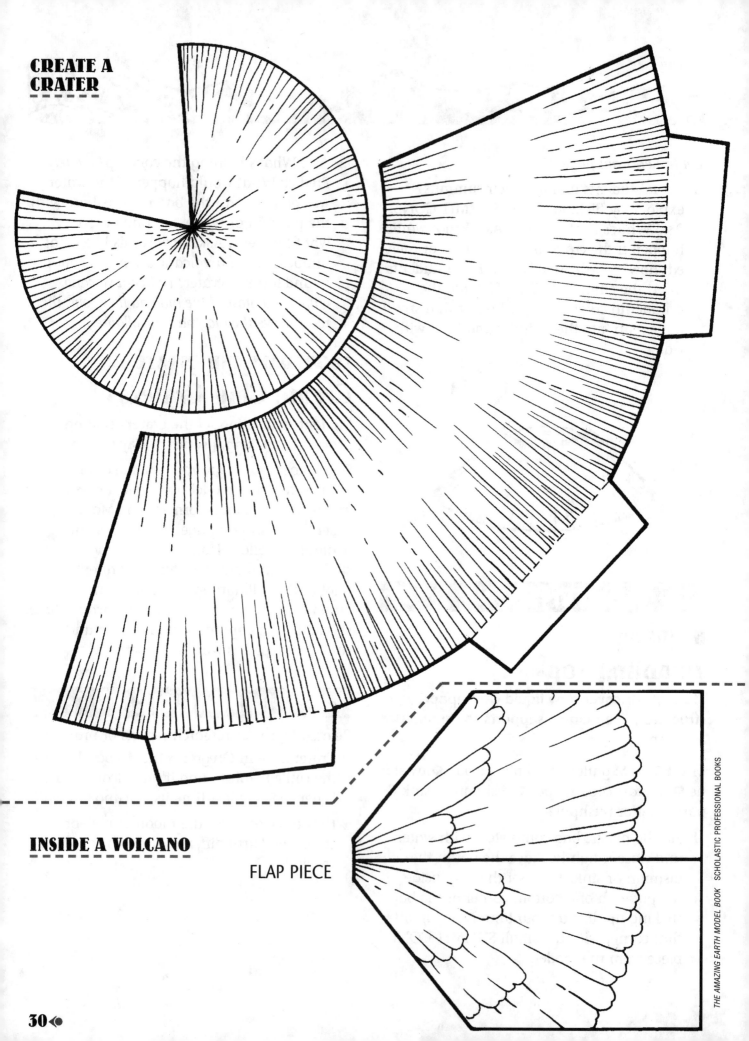

# CREATE A CRATER

## INSIDE A VOLCANO

FLAP PIECE

# CREATE A CRATER

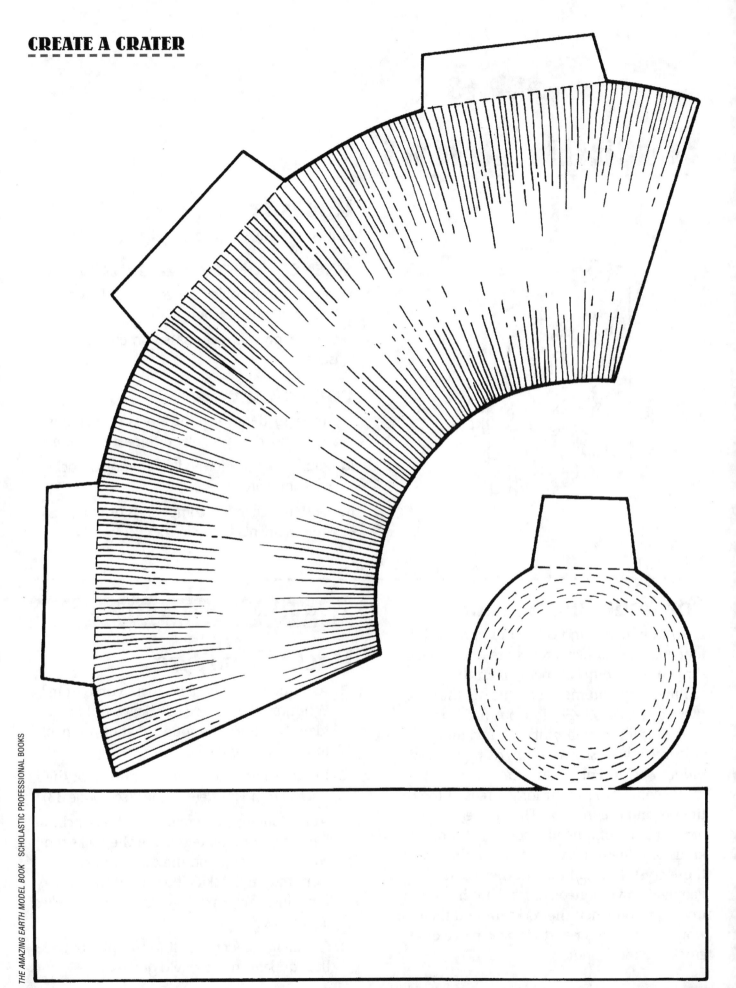

# Volcanic Rocks

## Rocks From Fire

Students make an igneous rock field guide.

### SCIENCE CONCEPTS & OBJECTIVES

• Infer that hot liquid rock cools and hardens into solid igneous rock

• Classify igneous rocks based on their characteristics

### VOCABULARY

**crystal** a solid in which the atoms or molecules are arranged in a regular or repeating pattern

**igneous rock** rock formed when molten rock cools and hardens

**mineral** the chemical compounds or solid, single elements found in rocks

## For Your Information

Lava from a volcano cools and hardens into igneous rock. Igneous rocks are one of the three main groups of rocks on Earth—sedimentary and metamorphic are the other two (see pages 37–49). Igneous rocks are formed from molten material, including volcanic lava, ash, or bombs as well as cooled magma below Earth's surface.

Volcanic rocks cover large areas of the continents and ocean floor. The differences among types of igneous rocks result from the kinds of mineral crystals in them, the size of those crystals, and how fast they cooled. People discover igneous rocks that hardened underground when the rocks around them are worn away or after earthquakes move or crack the rocks apart.

## TEACHING WITH THE MODEL

## Rocks From Fire

1. Ask students: Where do rocks come from? What are they made of? How would you identify a rock you found? What happens to lava after it cools?

2. Invite students to assemble and color their Rocks From Fire field guides (see page 33).

3. After students have read their books, challenge them to make a list of the rocks that came from lava and the ones that came from magma. Ask: What do all the rocks have in common? *(They were all once melted liquid rock.)*

4. Challenge students to find samples of rocks that appear in their field guides.

# Making the Model ✂

## Rocks From Fire

**MATERIALS:** reproducible pages 35 and 36 ◉ scissors ◉ stapler ◉ crayons, colored pencils, or markers

1. Photocopy pages 35 and 36.

2. Fold each page in half along the horizontal dotted line. The printed sides should be on the outside.

3. Next, fold each page in half again, as shown. Make sure the first booklet has the title page on its front and page 8 on its back, and the second booklet has page 3 on its front and page 6 on its back.

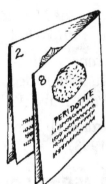

4. Nest the two booklets together. Check the page order—pages 4 and 5 should be in the book's center.

5. Staple the pages in the middle, as shown.

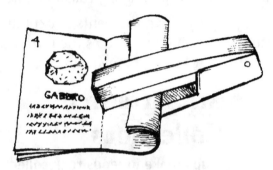

6. Color each rock's picture using information about it from its description in the field guide.

---

## EXTENSIONS

### HANDS-ON
# Rocky Meltdown

**Students observe how different solids melt, flow, and resolidify on cooling.**

Extreme heat and pressure inside Earth can melt rocks into magma. But different minerals melt and resolidify into crystals at different rates and temperatures. In this activity, students time different solids' rates of melting and resolidifying.

**MATERIALS:** butter or margarine ◉ chocolate or butterscotch chips ◉ marshmallows ◉ 3 pots ◉ stove or hot plate ◉ potholders

1. Place each ingredient in its own pot. Divide students into groups and assign each an ingredient. Turn the stove or hot plate to high and let it heat up. Tell students to stay away from the heating element.

2. Set a pot on the stove and say "Go." That ingredient's group times how long the solid takes to melt and records the time.

3. As soon as the ingredient is melted, remove it from the heat and set it on a safe surface. Ask the group to time how long it takes for the solid to resolidify and record the time. Be sure students do not touch the pots or the hot ingredients.

4. Continue until all the groups and ingredients have been melted and have had a chance to resolidify. (NOTE: You can use a

microwave instead of a stove. Heat the ingredients in microwave-safe bowls on high at 15-second intervals until melted.)

5. When all the ingredients have been tested, ask groups to compare times. What melted first? What melted last? How did each change on melting? Which ingredient re-solidified first? Last? What could be done to lessen the resolidification times? *(drop temperature by putting ingredient in a freezer)*

6. Wrap up by asking students to explain how this activity simulates the formation of different kinds of igneous rocks.

## COOPERATE AND COLLECT
# Rock Collections

**Student groups make igneous rock collections.**

Challenge student groups to collect as many different kinds of igneous rocks as they can. Invite them to label each with a description and display the collections in the classroom.

## RESEARCH IT

Related topics for research reports or projects:

◆ Molten rock that cools quickly on Earth's surface becomes extrusive igneous rock, while rock that cools slowly below Earth's surface becomes intrusive igneous rock. How are these two kinds of rock different? Which type has larger mineral crystals? Why?

◆ Granite is used to make stone buildings, and people use pumice to clean skin. What other kinds of igneous rock have commercial uses?

## VOLCANO RESOURCES

### BOOKS FOR STUDENTS
*Mountains and Volcanoes* by Barbara Taylor (Kingfisher, 1993)

*Volcano: The Eruption and Healing of Mount St. Helens* by Patricia Lauber (Bradbury Press, 1986)

*Volcanoes* by Jacqueline Dineen (Gloucester Press, 1991)

### BOOKS FOR TEACHERS
*Fire on the Mountain: The Nature of Volcanoes* by Dorian Weisel (Chronicle Books, 1994)

*Volcanoes: Mind-Boggling Experiments You Can Turn Into Science Fair Projects* by Janice VanCleave (Wiley, 1994)

*Volcanoes* by Gregory Vogt (Franklin Watts, 1993)

### OTHER RESOURCES
*Scholastic's The Magic School Bus Explores Inside the Earth* Windows CD-ROM (Microsoft Home, 1996)

*Volcanoes: Life on the Edge* Mac/Windows CD-ROM (Corbis, 1995)

*What's the Earth Made Of?* Video (National Geographic Educational Technology, 1995)

## TUFF

Tiny bits of lava and ash that get shot out of a volcano can become stuck together. When these particles cool and harden, they make tuff. Often other minerals fill in the holes in tuff. Tuff is pinkish-tan in color.

## OBSIDIAN
### ob-SI-dee-un

When lava cools very quickly, it can harden into glassy, black obsidian. Native Americans made arrowheads out of this rock. It breaks easily into pieces with sharp edges.

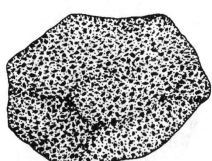

## PERIDOTITE
### peh-RIH-duh-tite

This dark green or black rock forms inside Earth's crust from magma. It contains a lot of iron. In South Africa, diamonds have been found in peridotite rocks.

# Rocks From Fire
## IGNEOUS ROCKS

# PUMICE
### PUH-miss

When pumice forms from lava, gas bubbles are trapped inside. When the bubbles burst, the rock is left looking "spongy." Pumice can be so light that it floats on water. It's a light gray color.

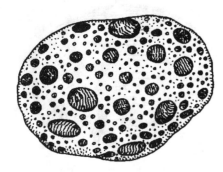

# GRANITE
### GRA-nit

Tough, hard granite rock is used in buildings and monuments. It is made of mineral crystals: white quartz, pink feldspar, and black mica. Granite hardens inside Earth's crust from magma. If it hardens quickly, it has small crystals. If it hardens slowly, the crystals are larger.

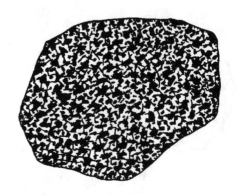

# GABBRO
### GA-brow

Gabbro forms from magma inside Earth's crust. It may take the magma thousands of years before it cools and hardens into gabbro. Gabbro can be dark green, dark gray, brown, or black.

# BASALT
### buh-SALT

As lava cools, it most often hardens into dark basalt. This common rock covers thousands of square miles of Earth's surface. In some places it is thousands of feet thick. The land in the country of Iceland is mostly made of basalt. This rock is dark reddish-brown.

# Sedimentary Rocks

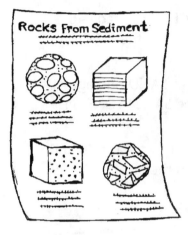

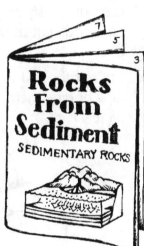

## Rocks From Sediment

Students model how sedimentary rocks form and make a sedimentary rock field guide.

### SCIENCE CONCEPTS & OBJECTIVES

➤ Infer how sediment forms sedimentary rocks

➤ Identify several examples of sedimentary rocks

### VOCABULARY

**sediment**  weathered rocks, shells, or minerals carried and deposited by water, wind, or ice

**sedimentary rock**  rock that forms from layers of sediment

## For Your Information

Most of the rocks found on Earth's surface are sedimentary rocks. Sedimentary rock is made of layers of sediment that have been pressed and/or cemented together. Weathered rocks and minerals—pebbles, sand, silt, or clay—are sediments. (See Rocks Under Attack, page 60, for more.) Animal remains such as shells or bones can be sediments too. All these sediments are washed via streams and rivers into lakes and oceans. Underwater they begin to pile up, each added layer weighing down the layer underneath it. Over time, the pressure of the piling layers presses the sediments together into rock. Sedimentary rock also forms when sediment layers are cemented together with minerals that fill tiny spaces between the sediments.

## TEACHING WITH THE MODEL

## Rocks From Sediment

1. Ask students: What is sediment? Give some examples. *(sand, pebbles, silt, clay, mud, shells)* What eventually happens to sand, pebbles, and other sediments? *(They continue to weather and/or are washed into the ocean.)*

2. Invite students to construct the Rocks From Sediment poster (see pages 40 and 41).

3. Explain that rivers carry sediments to the ocean. Large pebbles sink closest to shore, but sand, silt, and clay settle farther out. Ask: Why? *(Lighter sediments go farther.)* As sediments sink, they layer one on top of

# Making the Model

## Rocks From Sediment

**MATERIALS:** reproducible pages 40 and 41 ◉ crayons, colored pencils, or markers ◉ scissors ◉ glue or tape ◉ stapler

1. Photocopy pages 40 and 41.

2. Color the sediments on page 40.

3. Cut out the PEBBLES on page 40 along the thick black lines.

4. Glue or tape the PEBBLES to the CONGLOMERATE rock on the Rocks From Sediment poster, page 41.

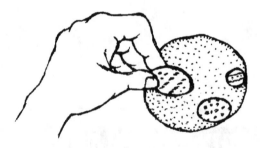

5. Cut out the ROCK CHIPS on page 40 and glue or tape them to the BRECCIA on page 41.

6. Cut out the square of SAND on page 40 tape or glue it to the SANDSTONE on page 41.

7. Cut out the MUD strips on page 40 and tape or glue them to the SHALE on page 41.

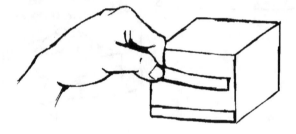

8. Photocopy pages 42 and 43 and assemble the Rocks From Sediment field guide following the instructions for the Rocks From Fire field guide on page 33.

another. The upper layers thicken and press on the lower layers. Some sediments are pressed so tightly they stick together. Others are pressed less tightly, leaving spaces that fill with minerals in seawater. The minerals cement the layers together into sedimentary rock.

4. Invite students to make the Rocks From Sediments field guide (see Making the Model, step 8, above).

5. After students have read their books, challenge them to make a list of the sedimentary rocks and write what kind of sediment created each.

6. Encourage students to find actual samples of the rocks that appear in their books.

## HANDS-ON
# Settling Down

**Students investigate how different kinds of sediments settle into layers.**

**MATERIALS:** sand ◉ silt ◉ gravel ◉ pebbles ◉ empty clear gallon jar with lid ◉ water

1. Place a small amount of sand, silt, gravel, and pebbles into the jar and fill it nearly full with water.

2. Cover and shake carefully. Ask: What will happen when I stop shaking and let the jar sit? Which sediments will settle first? Why?

3. Have students observe and note the sequence of sediment settling. Challenge students to draw a picture of the layers in the jar and label them. Ask: What would happen to the lower layers if the upper layers kept piling on? *(They would be pressed together, and the water would be squeezed out of them.)* What kind of rock forms like this? *(sedimentary rock)*

## COOPERATE AND COLLECT
# Rock Collections

**Student groups make sedimentary rock collections.**

Challenge students to collect as many different kinds of sedimentary rocks as they can. Invite them to label each with a description and display the collection in the classroom. Compare the rocks to the igneous rocks students found.

Related topics for research reports or projects:

◉ What are the different kinds of coal and where are they found?

◉ If sedimentary rocks form underwater, why are most of the rocks on Earth's dry surface sedimentary?

◉ The Grand Canyon's walls are made of many layers of sedimentary rocks. What are the different kinds of rock found there?

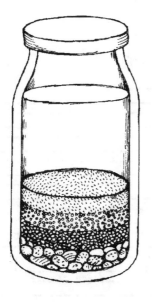

# ROCKS FROM SEDIMENT

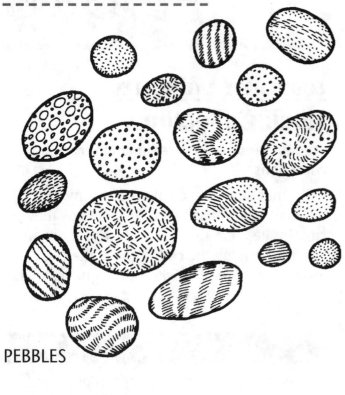

PEBBLES

ROCK CHIPS

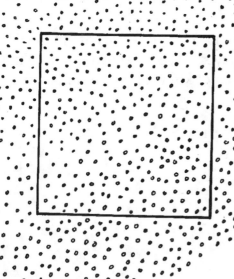

SAND

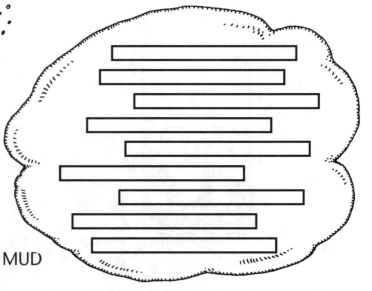

MUD

# Rocks From Sediment

Sedimentary rocks are formed from layers of sediment that have been pressed together.

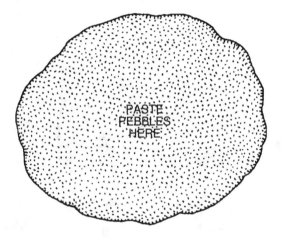

Conglomerate rock is made of different colored pebbles pressed and cemented together.

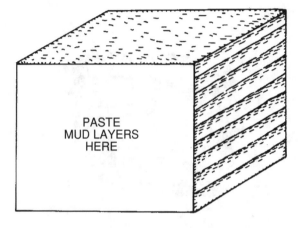

Shale is made of many thin, tightly packed layers of hardened mud.

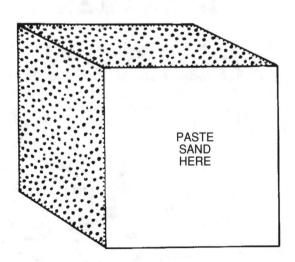

Sandstone is made of layers of sand compacted into rock.

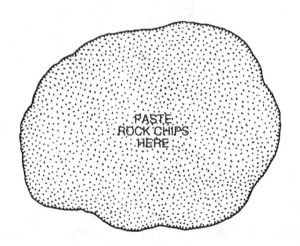

Breccia is made of rock chips cemented together.

## COAL

Shiny, black coal isn't formed from pebbles or sand. It's made of dead plants. Heat and pressure turned the dead plants into coal millions of years ago. Coal is burned to produce electricity.

## SHALE

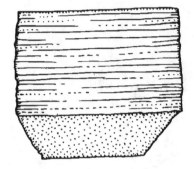

Shale is a sedimentary rock made up of layers of silt and clay. The green-gray layers can be split apart easily. Shale is used to make bricks.

## CONGLOMERATE
**kun-GLAH-muh-rate**

Find conglomerate rock and you will see different-colored, rounded pebbles cemented together. Conglomerate is a sedimentary rock sometimes used to make concrete.

# Rocks From Sediment
## SEDIMENTARY ROCKS

## LIMESTONE

The lime in limestone isn't a fruit but the mineral calcite. Sea creatures take calcite from seawater and use it to make their shells. After the creatures die, their shells sink and may become cemented into gray limestone.

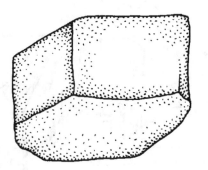

## BRECCIA
### BREH-chee-uh

Breccia is made up of multicolored rock chips cemented together. Often breccia forms from piles of broken rocks at the bottom of cliffs.

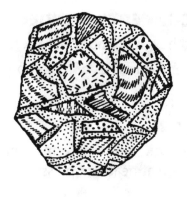

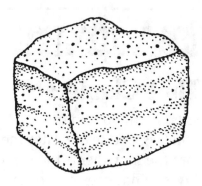

# SANDSTONE

When you touch sandstone, it feels gritty. It should, because this sedimentary rock forms from grains of sand cemented together by hardened minerals. Orange sandstone is used for building.

# CHALK

Chalk is a pure white form of limestone. Most school chalk these days isn't made out of the rock chalk. It's made of mineral powder glued together.

# Metamorphic Rocks

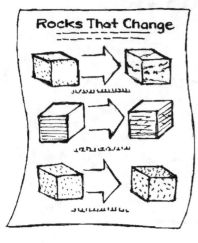

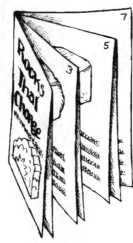

## Rocks That Change

Students model how metamorphic rocks form and make a metamorphic rock field guide.

### SCIENCE CONCEPTS & OBJECTIVES

➡ Understand how metamorphic rock forms

➡ Identify several examples of metamorphic rocks

### VOCABULARY

**metamorphic rock**  rock that forms from other rocks under great heat and pressure

## For Your Information

Rocks changed by intense heat and pressure while inside Earth's crust are called metamorphic rocks. The rocks' minerals and structure are altered as they change to metamorphic rock. Metamorphic rocks can form from sedimentary, igneous, or even other metamorphic rocks. If the sedimentary rock limestone is heated by surrounding magma underground, it can turn into marble (a metamorphic rock). Granite—an igneous rock—can change into the metamorphic rock gneiss under high heat and pressure. Intense pressure can change the sedimentary rock shale into slate, also a metamorphic rock. And if hot magma heats the slate, it could change again into hornfels, a different metamorphic rock.

## TEACHING WITH THE MODEL

## Rocks That Change

1. Ask students: What goes in a salad? *(lettuce, tomatoes, and so on)* After the salad is made, are the ingredients the same as at the start? *(yes)* What goes in a cake? *(flour, sugar, milk)* After the cake is baked, are the ingredients the same as at the start? *(No, they are different. They are now part of something new, a "cake.")* How is baking a cake like making metamorphic rocks? *(Ingredients change to make something new.)*

2. Remind students that metamorphic rocks form from igneous, sedimentary, or other metamorphic rocks under great heat and pressure in Earth's crust.

*(continued on page 46)*

# Making the Model

## Rocks That Change

**MATERIALS:** reproducible page 47 ◉ crayons ◉ scissors ◉ glue or tape ◉ colored pencils or markers ◉ stapler

1. Make two photocopies of page 47.

2. On one copy, use crayons to lightly color the LIMESTONE gray, the SHALE green-gray, and the SANDSTONE light red. (Lightly shading with the side of a crayon works well.) Cut out the three colored cubes.

3. Make MARBLE out of LIMESTONE. Wad up the cut-out gray LIMESTONE cube into a very tight ball. Press on the ball to represent pressure and make creases.

4. Now open and spread the cube out flat. Rub the side of a black crayon over the cube. This represents heat and brings out the crease patterns. The MARBLE should have dark veins.

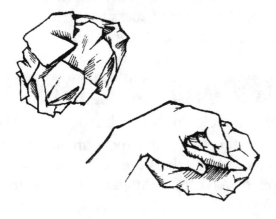

5. Tape or glue the finished MARBLE in the box next to the LIMESTONE on the other copy of page 47. This will become the Rocks That Change poster.

6. Make SLATE out of SHALE. Fold the greenish SHALE cube like an accordion. Make the folds in the same direction as the lines printed on the SHALE. Repeat step 4 to bring out the SHALE'S layers and attach it to the poster.

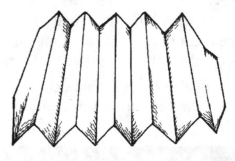

7. Make QUARTZITE from SANDSTONE. Gently wrinkle the reddish SANDSTONE cube. Repeat step 4 to enhance the QUARTZITE'S pattern and attach it to the poster.

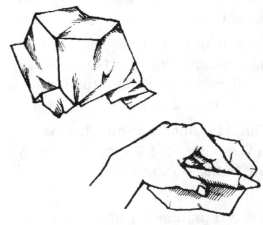

8. Reproduce pages 48 and 49 and assemble the Rocks That Change field guide following the instructions for the Rocks From Fire field guide on page 33.

*(continued from page 44)*

3. Have students make the Rocks That Change poster (see page 47).

4. As they make their posters, emphasize what the assembly steps represent. For example, when students wad up their cutout limestone cube it represents pressure. Coloring with the side of a crayon represents heating the rock.

5. Invite students to make the Rocks That Change field guide (see page 45).

6. After students have read their books, challenge them to make a list of metamorphic rocks and list the rocks they form from.

7. Encourage students to find actual samples of the rocks that appear in their books.

## EXTENSIONS

### HANDS-ON
# Melt a Rock

**Students investigate the metamorphosing power of heat.**

In this activity, students explore how heat changes cooking ingredients to simulate how heat and pressure in Earth's crust change rocks into metamorphic rock.

**MATERIALS:** mini-marshmallows ⊙ chocolate chips ⊙ mixing bowl ⊙ spoon ⊙ creamy peanut butter ⊙ waxed paper ⊙ pan ⊙ hot plate

1. Mix 2 cups mini-marshmallows and 1 cup chocolate chips in a bowl. Add just enough peanut butter so it clumps together.

2. Invite students to form "rocks" out of the mixture and set them on the waxed paper.

3. Ask: What kind of rocks do you think these are? *(They are sedimentary. The sediments of*

*chocolate and marshmallow are cemented with the mineral peanut butter.)* Ask: Would the rocks change if they were heated?

4. Heat half of the "rocks" together in the pan at low heat until the marshmallows melt. You can stir the mixture, but it doesn't need to be evenly mixed, just melted. Then carefully pour or spoon out globs of the mixture onto waxed paper. Let them completely cool into metamorphic "rocks."

5. Set each of the metamorphic "rocks" next to an original sedimentary "rock." Ask: What kind of rocks are these new rocks? *(metamorphic)* Why? *(Their structure and form were changed by heat.)*

## COOPERATE AND COLLECT
# Rock Collections

**Student groups make metamorphic rock collections.**

Challenge students to collect as many different kinds of metamorphic rocks as they can. Invite them to label each with a description and display the collection in the classroom. Compare the rocks to the igneous and sedimentary rocks students found.

## RESEARCH IT

Related topics for research reports or projects:

➥ Some metamorphic rocks are foliated or layered, while others are nonfoliated or unlayered. What's the difference in how they were formed?

➥ What are some of the uses of metamorphic rocks such as slate and marble? What are gemstones? What kind of rock are they found in?

# Rocks That Change

Metamorphic rocks have been changed
by heat and pressure inside Earth.

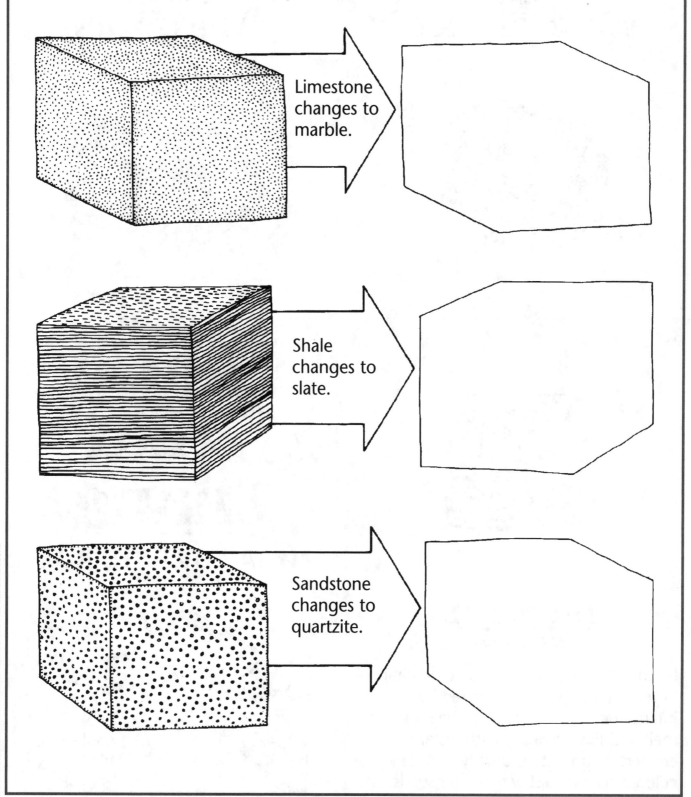

Limestone
changes to
marble.

Shale
changes to
slate.

Sandstone
changes to
quartzite.

## GRANITE GNEISS
### GRA-nit NICE

Under high heat and pressure, granite forms gneiss. Usually this metamorphic rock has bands of minerals and is speckled black and white. Sometimes the bands twist or curve, showing where the rock almost melted.

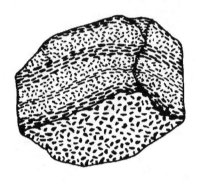

## 2

## MICA SCHIST
### MY-kuh SHIST

Gold-colored mica schist is a metamorphic rock that can form from shale. It can split into thinner layers than slate does.

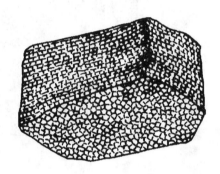

## MIGMATITE
### MIG-muh-tite

Migmatite is formed from a combination of rocks that have been melted by intense heat. When parts of the rocks melt and flow, swirling patterns are created. Migmatite is usually part dark-colored rock mixed with lighter swirls.

# Rocks That Change
## METAMORPHIC ROCKS

3

## SLATE

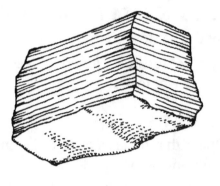

High pressure can change shale into slate. Slate is very hard and splits into flat sheets. That's why it is often used for chalkboards, roof tiles, and patio stones. Slate is usually dark blue-gray.

6

## QUARTZITE
### KWORT-site

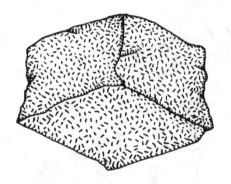

Sandstone under a lot of pressure deep inside Earth can end up changing to quartzite. It's a grayish tan color. Most quartzite is more than 500 million years old.

4

## HORNFELS
### HORN-felz

Hornfels comes from slate that was heated by nearby magma. It means "horn rock" in German. Hornfels looks like shiny, dark-brown horn.

5

## MARBLE
### MAR-bul

Intense heat from magma inside Earth's crust, or intense pressure, can change limestone into marble. Pure marble is white, but minerals in marble can color it pink, green, yellow, or black. Marble is used in building.

# Fossil Find

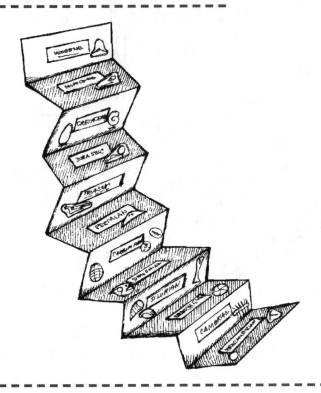

## Fossil Timeline

This model shows how fossils accumulate in distinct layers.

### SCIENCE CONCEPTS & OBJECTIVES

→ Understand what fossils are

→ Infer why older fossils are found in deeper layers than newer fossils

### VOCABULARY

**fossil** anything that remains of an organism that lived a long time ago

**paleontologist** a scientist that studies ancient life and fossils

**period** A unit of geological time. The number of years in a period varies.

## For Your Information

Fossils are the remains of animals and plants that lived long ago. Fossils can be unchanged ancient bones, teeth, and shells as well as wood that has petrified or bones that have filled with hardened minerals. Fossils can also be leaf outlines pressed into rock or footprints in hardened mud.

Fossil formation is the exception, not the rule. When most living things die, they are eaten or rot away without leaving a trace. But some plants and animal bodies are quickly buried in mud or sand. This cuts off the oxygen and stops normal decay. Though the soft body parts rot, harder parts remain. Over time, sediment layers pile up and eventually form sedimentary rocks that contain fossils inside. Digging up and studying fossils have taught scientists about ancient plants and animals and the history of life on Earth.

## TEACHING WITH THE MODEL

## Fossil Timeline

1. Ask students: Do dinosaurs and woolly mammoths live today? *(no)* How do we know they ever lived at all? *(fossil remains)* Why do you think most fossils are found in sedimentary rocks? *(buried by sediment)* What do you think would happen to fossils in fiery hot lava? *(burn up)*

2. Invite students to make the model (see page 51).

3. Review the names of the geological periods and life forms on the panels with students.

4. Ask students to imagine that the panels on their models are layers of sedimentary rocks in a canyon. Paleontologists often find fossils in such layers. Challenge

# Making the Model

## Fossil Timeline

**MATERIALS:** reproducible pages 53 and 54 ⊙ scissors ⊙ tape or glue ⊙ two colors of construction paper

1. Photocopy pages 53 and 54.

2. Cut 3 sheets of two colors of construction paper in half. You should end up with a total of 12 paper panels each about 8 by 5 inches, 6 of one color and 6 of another color.

3. Place the panels lengthwise, alternating colors and taping together, as shown.

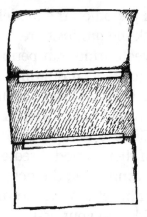

4. Cut out the 12 numbered rectangles on page 53 along the heavy black lines. Tape each rectangle onto its panel in numerical order, as shown.

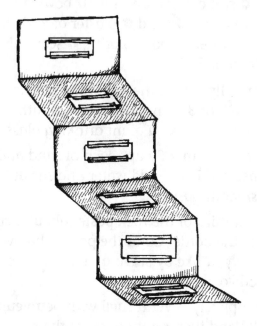

5. Cut out the fossils on page 54 and tape each onto the appropriate panel according to its label.

students to explain why the oldest fossils are in the lowest rock layers and more recent fossils in the higher layers. *(The presence of a fossil in a rock layer implies the organism that left the fossil died before the rock layer formed. Newer layers of sediment settle on top of older layers of sediment or on rocks already formed.)*

5. Challenge students to figure out what it means when certain fossils stop showing up in sedimentary rock layers. Hint: Would scientists find dinosaur fossils in sedimentary rocks that formed after the dinosaurs became extinct?

# EXTENSIONS

## HANDS-ON
# Lasting Impressions

**Students discover how imprints can be left behind in sedimentary rock layers.**

MATERIALS: empty plastic one-liter soda bottle ✪ scissors or craft knife ✪ bowl ✪ measuring cup ✪ sand ✪ plaster of Paris ✪ spoon ✪ water ✪ food coloring ✪ seashells ✪ petroleum jelly

1. Carefully cut off the top of the plastic bottle 2 or 3 inches below the mouth. It should look like a giant drinking glass.

2. In a bowl, mix 3 cups each of sand and plaster of Paris. Add water and stir until it's a smooth paste.

3. Put a third of the rock paste (about 2 cups) into the bottle. Color the paste whatever color you like by stirring in a few drops of food coloring.

4. Completely cover a shell with petroleum jelly and then set it on top of the rock paste in the bottle.

5. Add another third of the rock paste to the bottle and leave it uncolored.

6. Completely cover another shell or two with petroleum jelly and set it on top of this second layer of rock paste in the bottle.

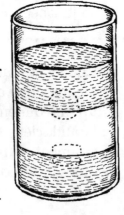

7. Color the remaining rock paste in the bowl a different color from the first layer. Pour it in the bottle to make a final layer. Dispose of any remaining paste in the trash. Do not wash it down the drain!

8. After a few days, the rock layers will be hard. Carefully cut away the bottle. Then dig for fossils by breaking open the layers and finding the shells and their imprints. Ask: Which is the fossil, the shells or their imprints? *(both)* If these were real rock layers, which shells would be the oldest? *(the ones on the bottom)*

GOING FURTHER: Challenge students to find present-day fossil-like imprints in sidewalk cement. What do they find? *(footprints, bird tracks, paw prints, initials, leaf prints)*

## COOPERATE AND CREATE
# Back in Time

**Students create their own timelines.**

Assign each period on the model to a group of students. Ask the groups to research what creatures lived during that period and challenge them to create a diorama or poster to represent their period. Have them include plant and animal life as well as inland seas or volcanoes. Be sure students indicate the name and dates of their period. Create a classroom timeline by connecting the posters in chronological order or setting the dioramas side by side from oldest to youngest.

# RESEARCH IT

Related topics for research reports or projects:
➨ How do scientists date fossils?
➨ What do the La Brea tar pits have to do with fossils?
➨ What is amber and what kinds of fossils have been found in it?

| | |
|---|---|
| **NEOGENE** [12]<br>24 million years ago to present | **CARBONIFEROUS** [6]<br>360–286 million years ago |
| **PALEOGENE** [11]<br>65–24 million years ago | **DEVONIAN** [5]<br>408–360 million years ago |
| **CRETACEOUS** [10]<br>144–65 million years ago | **SILURIAN** [4]<br>438–408 million years ago |
| **JURASSIC** [9]<br>213–144 million years ago | **ORDOVICIAN** [3]<br>505–438 million years ago |
| **TRIASSIC** [8]<br>248–213 million years ago | **CAMBRIAN** [2]<br>590–505 million years ago |
| **PERMIAN** [7]<br>286–248 million years ago | **PRECAMBRIAN** [1]<br>650–590 million years ago |

# FOSSIL TIMELINE

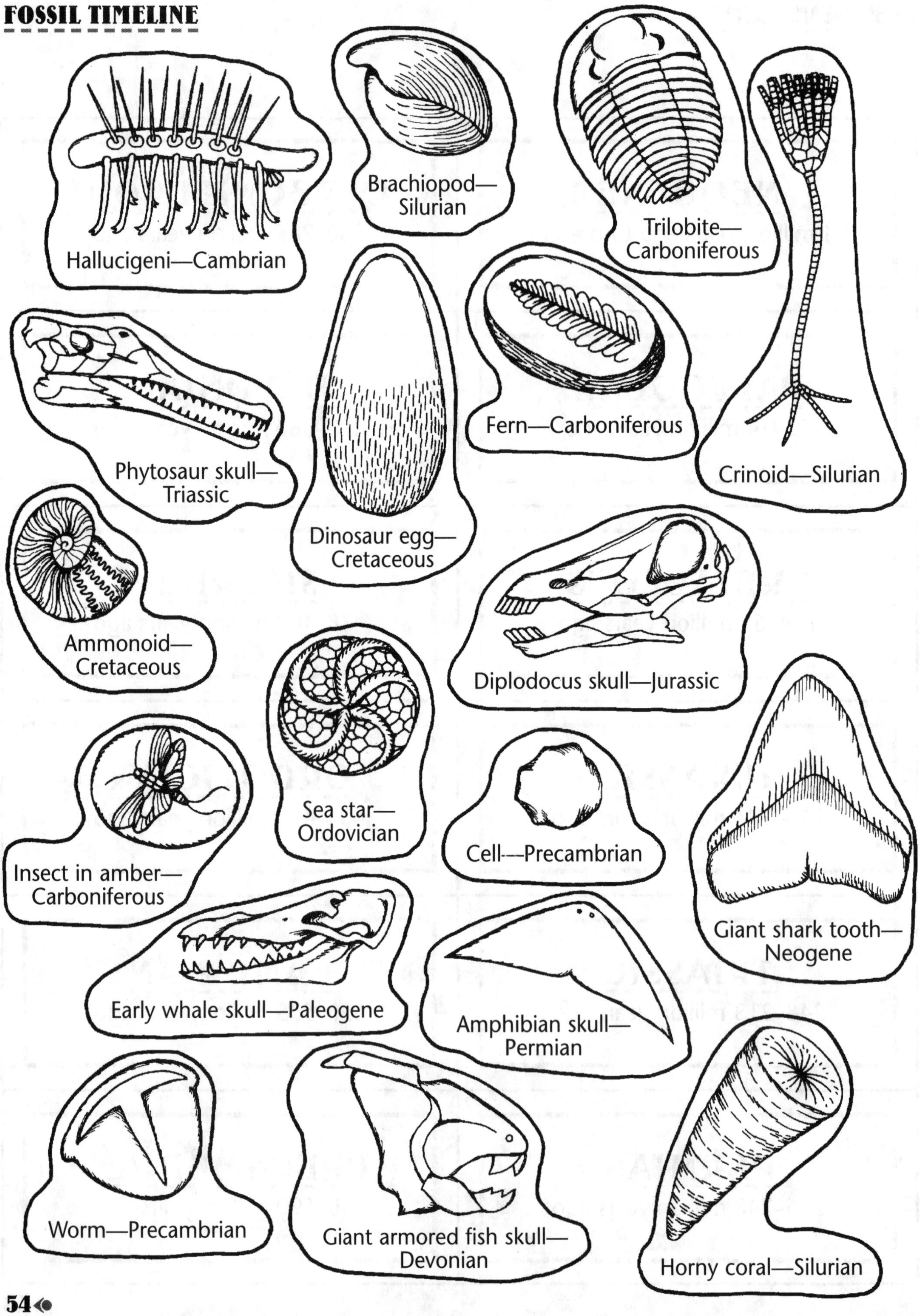

Hallucigeni—Cambrian

Brachiopod—Silurian

Trilobite—Carboniferous

Crinoid—Silurian

Phytosaur skull—Triassic

Dinosaur egg—Cretaceous

Fern—Carboniferous

Ammonoid—Cretaceous

Diplodocus skull—Jurassic

Insect in amber—Carboniferous

Sea star—Ordovician

Cell—Precambrian

Giant shark tooth—Neogene

Early whale skull—Paleogene

Amphibian skull—Permian

Worm—Precambrian

Giant armored fish skull—Devonian

Horny coral—Silurian

THE AMAZING EARTH MODEL BOOK  SCHOLASTIC PROFESSIONAL BOOKS

# The Rock Cycle

## Rock Recycle Wheel

This model depicts how rocks form from other rocks.

### SCIENCE CONCEPTS & OBJECTIVES

- Understand how rocks form, are broken down, and form other rocks
- Infer that the rock cycle continually produces and recycles rock
- Review how igneous, sedimentary, and metamorphic rocks form

### VOCABULARY

**moving plates**  the thick rigid pieces of Earth's crust

**rock cycle**  the never-ending process of rocks forming, weathering, and changing into other rocks

## For Your Information

The rock cycle is a never-ending process. Igneous rock forms from magma or lava. Weathering breaks igneous rock into sediments that are compacted and cemented into sedimentary rock. Under great heat and pressure inside Earth's crust, igneous and sedimentary rocks are changed into metamorphic rocks. Metamorphic rocks are also changed into new kinds of metamorphic rock. Like igneous rock, sedimentary and metamorphic rock also weather into sediments that in turn can become sedimentary rock and subsequently metamorphic rock. The rock cycle comes full circle when moving plates melt and pull rock deep inside Earth's crust. There the rock changes into magma once again.

## TEACHING WITH THE MODEL

## Rock Recycle Wheel

1. Ask students: Where do rocks come from? *(Invite students to review what they've learned about igneous, sedimentary, and metamorphic rocks.)* Why doesn't Earth run out of magma for making igneous rock? *(Rocks are continually melted into "new" magma by moving plates.)* (See page 110.)

2. Invite students to make the model (see page 56).

3. Ask students to turn the circles until IGNEOUS shows in the notch on the circle's outer rim. Granite will show in the top window. Ask: What kind of rock is granite?

# Making the Model

## Rock Recycle Wheel

**MATERIALS:** reproducible pages 58 and 59 ⊙ scissors ⊙ brass fasteners ⊙ crayons, colored pencils, or markers

1. Photocopy pages 58 and 59.

2. Cut out the circle on page 59 along the heavy black line. Color the rocks and sediments on this page, if you like.

3. Cut out the circle with the notch on page 58. Then cut out its three windows.

4. Stack the notched circle on top of the other circle. Punch a brass fastener

through the hole in the center to hold the circles together.

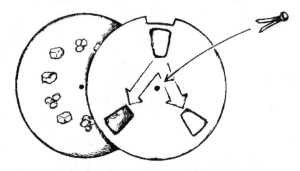

5. Color the rocks using information from your rock field guides.

---

*(igneous, as reads in notch)* How does granite form? Allow students to use their rock books to find the answer. *(Granite forms from magma cooling underground.)* What happens when granite weathers? Instruct students to follow the arrow to find out. *(It turns to pebbles, as shown in lower right window.)* Ask: What happens to granite under great heat and pressure? Again instruct students to follow the arrow to find out. *(It forms the metamorphic rock gneiss, as shown in lower left window.)*

4. Repeat with SEDIMENTS, SEDIMENTARY, and METAMORPHIC. (Be sure students understand that pebbles weather to smaller pieces of sediment but can also form metamorphic rock.) Note: IGNEOUS, SEDIMENTS, SEDIMENTARY, and METAMORPHIC must appear in the notch above the top window for the other windows to be correct. Any other combinations are incorrect.

## EXTENSIONS

### HANDS-ON
## Minute Rice

**Students generate heat through friction.**

Friction between moving crustal plates heats and melts rock. This activity allows students to experience how friction generates heat.

**MATERIALS:** jar with lid ⊙ uncooked rice (birdseed works well too) ⊙ thermometer

1. Fill the jar with 2 to 3 inches of rice or seed.

2. Place a thermometer in the rice and record the temperature. (Wait at least a minute to get an accurate reading.)

3. Take out the thermometer and cap the jar.

4. Shake the jar continuously and vigorously for 1 to 2 minutes.

5. Quickly uncap the jar and immediately take the rice's temperature again. Record it. Ask: What happened? *(The temperature rose.)* Why? *(Friction created by the rice grains rubbing together made heat.)* How is this like what happens to rocks where plates move against each other? *(The plates rubbing against each other also create friction, which melts rock.)*

## COOPERATE AND CREATE
# This Is Your Life, Rock

**Student groups create a cartoon life history for a rock.**

Divide students into groups and assign each a type of sediment—silt, sand, pebbles, or rock chips. Challenge each group to write and illustrate a cartoon life story for their sediment. For example, they could explain how it became a sedimentary rock, then a metamorphic rock, then was melted into magma and reborn as an igneous rock. Encourage students to identify what kind of rock (marble, sandstone, etc.) it became at each stage. Invite them to color and then bind their stories into comic books to be shared with the rest of the class.

## RESEARCH IT

Related topics for research reports or projects:

- At what temperature do rocks change back into magma?
- How long does it take for a rock to change back into magma?
- Does the moon have a rock cycle? How do we know?

## ROCKS & FOSSILS RESOURCES

### BOOKS FOR STUDENTS

*Eyewitness Explorers: Rocks and Minerals* by Steve Parker (Dorling Kindersley, 1993)

*One Small Square: Swamp* by Donald M. Silver and Patricia J. Wynne (McGraw-Hill, 1997)

*Rocks* by Terry Jennings (Garrett, 1991)

*Rocks & Minerals at Your Fingertips* by Judy Nayer (McClanahan, 1995)

### BOOKS FOR TEACHERS

*Eyewitness Books: Rocks & Minerals* by R. F. Symes (Knopf, 1988)

*Rocks & Fossils* by Ray Oliver (Random House, 1993)

*Rocks and Minerals: Mind-Boggling Experiments You Can Turn Into Science Fair Projects* by Janice VanCleave (Wiley, 1996)

### OTHER RESOURCES

*Geology: Rocks and Minerals* Mac/Windows CD-ROM (National Geographic Educational Technology, 1994)

*Message in a Fossil* Mac/PC CD-ROM (Steck-Vaughn, 1996)

heat and pressure

weathering

**Rock Recycle Wheel**

THE AMAZING EARTH MODEL BOOK   SCHOLASTIC PROFESSIONAL BOOKS

# ROCK RECYCLE WHEEL

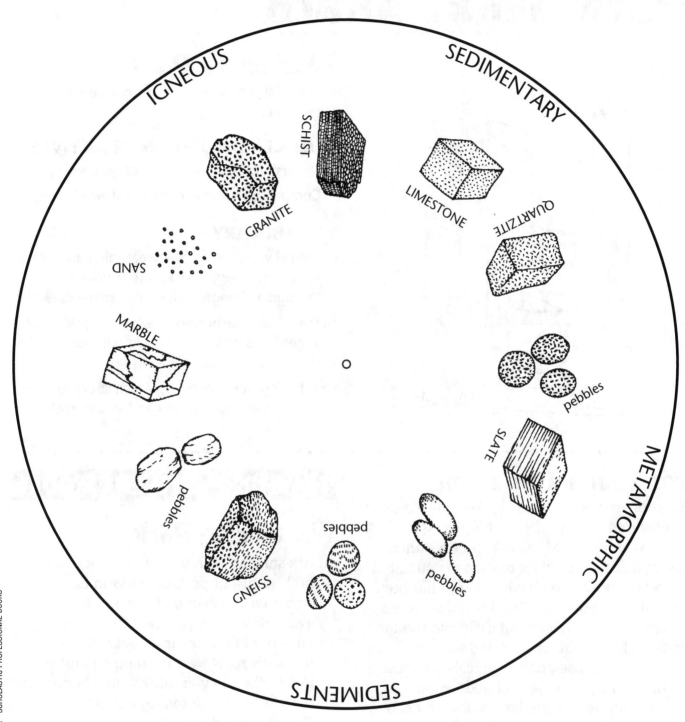

# Rocks Under Attack

## Weathering Park

This model shows where and how weathering takes place.

### SCIENCE CONCEPTS & OBJECTIVES

- Understand how the agents of weathering work
- Compare physical and chemical weathering

### VOCABULARY

**chemical weathering**  the weakening and breaking down of larger rocks into smaller rocks through a change in the rocks' minerals

**mechanical weathering**  the breaking down of larger rocks into smaller rocks without changing the rocks' minerals

**weathering**  the process by which larger rocks are broken down into smaller and smaller rocks

## For Your Information

Rocks are constantly being broken down into smaller and smaller pieces. This process is called weathering. Most of the time weathering takes place too slowly for anyone to notice. But nearly every rock you have ever seen has been shaped by weathering. Over time, this process flattens mountains, cuts out cliffs, and changes boulders into grains of sand and soil.

Water, ice, gases, and chemicals are some of the agents—or causes—of weathering. Mechanical weathering breaks down rocks by force—plant roots pushing into rock, rocks freezing and thawing, wind blowing sand against rocks, for example. Chemical weathering breaks down rocks by chemically changing the rocks' minerals. This weakens them, and the rocks crumble.

## TEACHING WITH THE MODEL

## Weathering Park

1. Ask students: What do you think causes nails to rust or potholes to form in streets? *(corrosion and wear and tear, which are like weathering)* Have you ever seen a plant grow out of a crack in a rock? Do you think the roots were pushing against the rock? What do you think would happen if the roots kept thickening and pushing? *(The rock would break.)*

2. Invite students to make the model (see page 61) and color it.

*(continued on page 62)*

# Making the Model

## Weathering Park

**MATERIALS:** reproducible pages 64–66 ⊙ scissors ⊙ tape ⊙ crayons, colored pencils, or markers

1. Photocopy pages 64–66.

2. Cut out the large rectangle on page 64.

3. Cut open all four of the flaps along their three heavy black lines. One side of each rectangle will remain uncut. HINT: Fold the paper, snip an opening, and insert the scissors to more easily cut out the flaps.

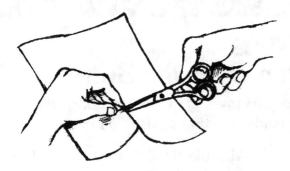

4. Fold back each flap along the dashed line, crease well, and then close.

5. Repeat steps 2 to 4 for page 65.

6. Repeat step 2 for page 66.

7. Stack all three rectangles on top of one another. They should be in the same order as their original pages, as shown.

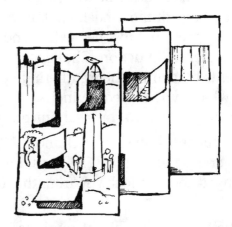

8. Line up all the edges and hold while taping together, as shown. By overlapping the tape from the top page to the bottom page, the middle page will be sandwiched inside.

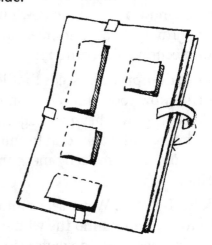

*(continued from page 60)*

3. Point out that there are two main kinds of weathering: mechanical and chemical. In mechanical weathering, rocks are broken into smaller and smaller pieces but the minerals in the rocks remain unchanged. In chemical weathering, the minerals in rocks are changed or dissolved away. As a result of these changes, the rocks weaken and eventually crumble.

4. Ask students to describe what they see on the top page of the model. Explain that by opening the top flaps they will see agents of weathering in action. Challenge students to identify the weathering agents and which type of weathering is occurring—chemical or mechanical.

5. After students have had a chance to think, go over each example. (The flaps are arranged counterclockwise from the top right.)

   ➤ **Obelisk.** As rain falls, it combines with carbon dioxide gas in the air and becomes a weak acid, like soda water. This acid can chemically change or dissolve away minerals in the obelisk's rock.

   ➤ **Cliff.** Cliff rocks wedged loose by plant roots or freezing water tumble down under the pull of gravity. Roots and freezing are agents of mechanical weathering.

   ➤ **Seeds near chipmunk.** Seeds that land in rocks can grow roots that reach into cracks. As roots grow, they push against rocks, enlarging old cracks and forming new ones. Roots split rocks by mechanical weathering.

   ➤ **Crack in the rock.** Water seeps into cracks in rocks, and during the winter it can freeze into ice. Freezing water expands and pushes open cracks even more. Such repeated freezing, thawing, and refreezing is called *frost action* and is an example of mechanical weathering.

6. Invite students to open the second inner flaps and challenge them to interpret the long-term effects of weathering such as: fallen rocks pile up at the foot of the cliff and continue weathering to rubble; the carvings on the obelisk are nearly worn away; cracks in rocks keep growing larger; the hillside crumbles.

7. Students can label each of the weathering agents and type of weathering on the top flaps.

## EXTENSIONS

### HANDS-ON
# Pop Goes the Bottle

**Students investigate how freezing water expands, exerting a pushing force.**

**MATERIALS:** plastic film canister (or plastic water or juice bottle with a push-close cap, not screw-on) ○ water ○ freezer

1. Fill the film canister with water. Make sure it's completely filled. Cap it and place in a freezer overnight.

2. Remove the film canister the next day. Ask: What happened? *(Ice pushed up the cap.)* Does frozen water take up more or less space than liquid water? *(more)* If the bottle were a rock, which kind of weathering would this be? *(mechanical)* Why? *(physical force broke the rock, not chemical change)*

## HANDS-ON
# When Acid Rains

**Students discover how acid rain affects stone structures.**

When pollution in the air mixes with water droplets in clouds, acid rain can form. This activity lets students see how acid rain affects statues and other kinds of stone structures.

MATERIALS: paper clip, bent open ◐ piece of chalk ◐ lump of clay ◐ saucer ◐ safety goggles ◐ eyedropper ◐ white vinegar

1. Have students make a "statue" by using the open paper clip to carve details in the chalk. They can use the clay to stand the statue upright in the saucer.

2. Wearing goggles, students then use the eyedropper to drop "acid rain" (the vinegar) over the statue. While continuing to make it rain, they should observe how the statue changes. *(The acid rain causes the statue to wear away.)* What kind of weathering would this be? *(chemical)* Why? *(Chemical change weakened the chalk. Calcium carbonate in chalk is chemically related to limestone and marble, building materials most affected by acid rain. Vinegar—acetic acid—is a substitue for the sulfuric and nitric acids in acid rain.)* NOTE: Vinegar is more acidic than acid rain. In reality, the effects of acid rain would not be visible for many years.

## COOPERATE AND CREATE
# Weathering Hunt

**Students find signs of weathering around them.**

Divide students into groups and go outside for a weathering hunt. Remind them that they don't need to limit themselves to weathering rocks—any kind of weathering will do. Rust on fences or cars, cracks in bricks, potholes, cracked shingles, and peeling paint are all good examples. Invite each group to make a list of as many weathering examples as they find. Encourage them to draw a picture of each example and label it as mechanical or chemical weathering.

## RESEARCH IT

Related topics for research reports or projects:

◆ What could cause mechanical weathering on the moon? *(meteorites hitting the moon's surface)* Why is there no chemical weathering there? *(no atmosphere)*

◆ How might chemicals given off by factory smokestacks affect weathering? *(They help create acid rain.)*

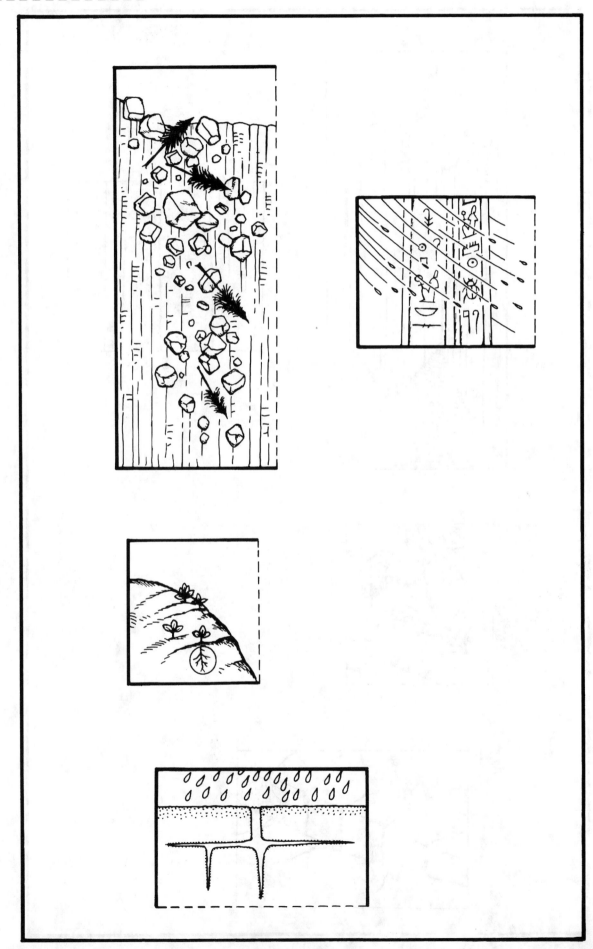

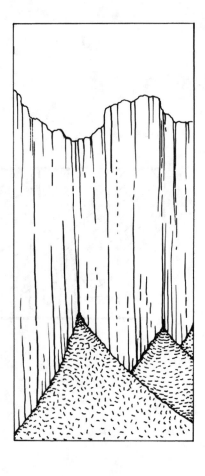

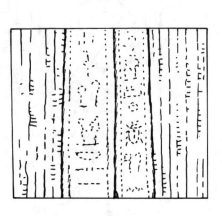

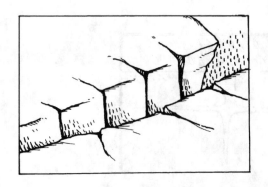

# The Story of Soil

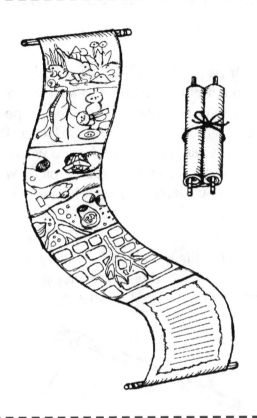

## Soil Layers Scroll

This model shows the three soil layers formed by weathering.

### SCIENCE CONCEPTS & OBJECTIVES

- Identify and compare the three soil layers
- Infer how soil life helps weathering occur

### VOCABULARY

**bedrock** unweathered rock found under soil

**humus** nutrient-rich decayed plants and animals

**subsoil** middle soil layer that contains minerals washed out of topsoil

**substratum** deepest soil layer where rocks weather to form new subsoil

**topsoil** the uppermost soil layer that contains humus

## For Your Information

Soil is made of bits and pieces of weathered rocks. It also contains minerals, water, air, and *humus*—decayed plants and animals. There are three soil layers: *topsoil, subsoil,* and *substratum.*

Most plants need soil to grow. Earthworms, moles, ants, and many other animals make their home in soil as well. As these creatures dig and tunnel, they loosen and mix the soil. They create spaces that let in air and allow water to percolate down to lower soil levels, where it causes further weathering of rock.

## TEACHING WITH THE MODEL

## Soil Layers Scroll

1. Ask students: Have you ever dug into the soil? What did you find? Then ask: How do our lives depend on soil? *(Plants need soil, and plants provide us with food, oxygen, and many other products.)* What creatures live in the soil?

2. Invite students to make the model (see page 68) and color it and the Soil Creatures and Plants (see page 73).

*(continued on page 69)*

# Making the Model

## Soil Layers Scroll

**MATERIALS:** reproducible pages 71–73 ☉ scissors ☉ tape ☉ crayons, colored pencils, or markers ☉ glue ☉ 2 unsharpened pencils ☉ string or ribbon

1. Photocopy pages 71 and 72.

2. Cut out the four rectangles on pages 71 and 72 along the heavy black lines.

3. Place the rectangles one above the other. The order top to bottom: Above Ground/Topsoil, Subsoil, Substratum, and Soil Scroll Script.

4. Now turn the rectangles facedown and tape them together on the back. The tape needs to reach and cover the edges, as shown.

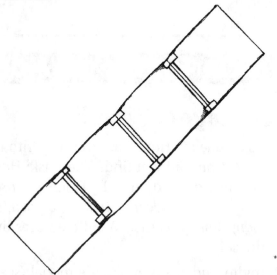

5. Color the soil. Soil comes in many colors— red, brown, yellow, gray. Think about soil and rocks you've seen and base the colors on your experience. Or, research this information.

6. Color page 73, Soil Creatures and Plants. Then cut out the plants and animals you want to use in your soil scrolls and tape or glue them in an appropriate soil level. The captions will give you clues as to where they belong. Complete your scroll by writing a script describing what happens in the lives of these underground plants and creatures.

7. Assemble the finished soil scroll by taking one unsharpened pencil and taping it to one end of the scroll, as shown.

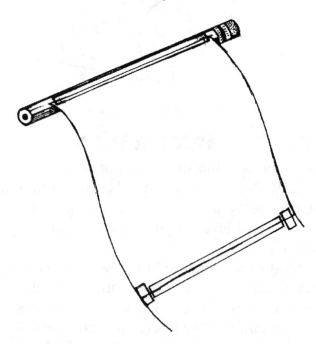

8. Repeat step 7 with the other pencil and scroll end. Then roll up the scroll from both ends and tie in the middle with string or ribbon.

*(continued from page 67)*

3. Point out each soil layer and discuss its characteristics with the class (see Soil Layers below). Also ask about the plants and creatures that possibly live there.

4. Now invite students to glue or tape some of the plants and creatures onto their soil scrolls, using the captions below each as a clue to its location. Then challenge students to write a story about what goes on in their scroll on the Soil Scroll Script at the end of their model.

---

# Soil Layers

➡ *Topsoil* is the top layer of soil. It is made of silt, clay, and other tiny pieces of rock produced by weathering. Topsoil usually contains nutrient-rich humus, which gives it a gray-black color. Most plants grow in topsoil, and many animals live there, too. Animals are agents of weathering. They loosen and mix topsoil, allowing air and water to filter down to lower soil layers. When dead plants and animals decay, they produce acids that also cause weathering.

➡ *Subsoil,* the second layer, is a lighter-colored soil layer because it contains little dark humus. Subsoil contains minerals washed out of topsoil by rain and melting snow. Subsoil contains larger pieces of weathered rock than topsoil. Some plant roots grow down into the subsoil in search of deep water.

➡ The third layer, the *substratum,* is where mostly large pieces of rock are being worn down by weathering to form new subsoil. Below the substratum is solid, hard, unweathered bedrock.

---

## EXTENSIONS

### HANDS-ON
# Soil Soak

**Students compare the water-holding ability of topsoil and sand.**

Topsoil holds a lot of water because it contains humus and other absorbent soil particles. Water also gets trapped in the spaces between the soil particles. This activity invites students to measure how much water topsoil and sand can each hold.

MATERIALS: 2 paper cups ◉ pencil ◉ sand ◉ potting soil ◉ 3 liquid measuring cups ◉ water

1. Carefully poke 10 small holes in the bottom of two paper cups with a sharp pencil.

2. Fill each cup two-thirds full—one with sand and the other with potting soil. Set each inside a liquid measuring cup.

3. Slowly pour one cup of water into each paper cup. Pick up the cups and hold them so they drain easily for two minutes.

4. Set the paper cups aside and measure how much water is in each measuring cup. Ask: Which measuring cup has more water? *(sand)* Which cup held more water? *(potting soil)* Why? *(Like topsoil, it contains humus and other absorbent materials.)* Why is this important? *(Plants need the water in the soil to grow.)*

## COOPERATE AND CREATE
# Dig It Up

Students observe what is in schoolyard soil and create a mini–soil profile in a jar.

**MATERIALS:** newspapers ⊙ glass or clear plastic jars ⊙ shovel ⊙ yardstick

1. Divide the class into small groups and give each group some newspaper and a jar. Students will need notebooks to record their findings.

2. Go into the schoolyard and dig up some soil. Place a shovelful on each group's newspaper and allow students to examine it. Ask: What color is it? Is it rough or smooth? Are there any creatures moving around in it?

3. Dig deeper into the soil. When the soil changes color, stop digging and measure how deep you are. This should be the beginning of the subsoil. Have students record this depth.

4. Dig into the subsoil and place shovelfuls on each group's newspaper. Ask: What color is it? Is it rough or smooth? Are there any creatures moving around in it? How is it different from the topsoil?

5. If possible, keep digging until you hit mostly rocks—the substratum—and allow students to observe this also. This may not be possible if your upper soil layers are very thick.

6. Now invite students to create a mini–soil profile. Have them fill their jars with layers of soil proportional to what they observed. Back in the classroom they can label the layers and their characteristics. After students have studied the contents of their jars, have them return the soil (and its inhabitants) where they found it.

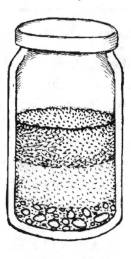

## RESEARCH IT

Related topics for research reports or projects:

⦿ How long does it take for an inch or centimeter of soil to form? In which climates does soil form fastest? Slowest? Why?

⦿ How do farmers prevent their soil from being washed away?

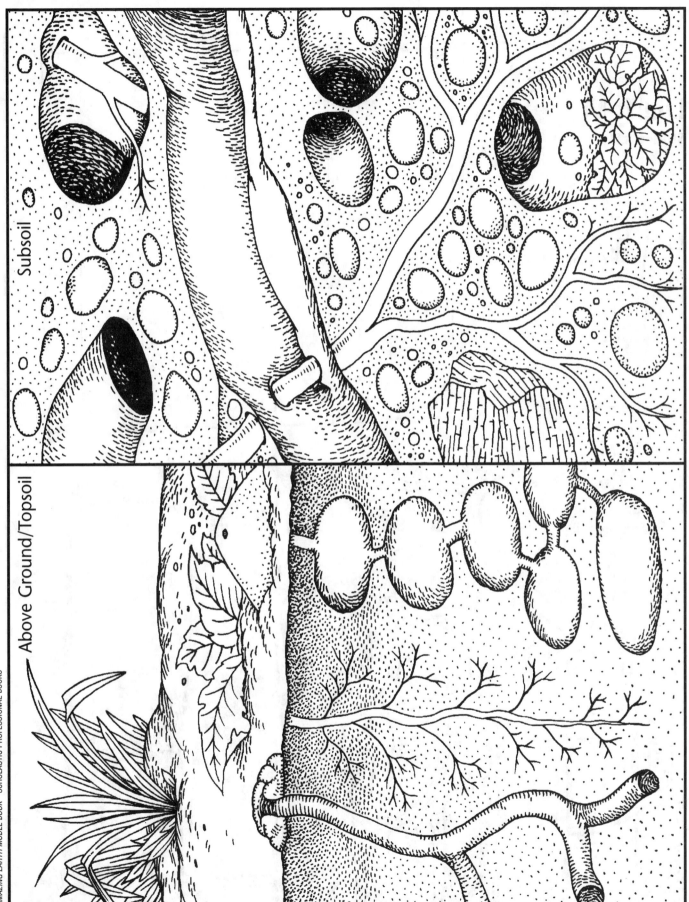

Subsoil

Above Ground/Topsoil

## SOIL SCROLL SCRIPT

Substratum

# SOIL CREATURES AND PLANTS

Moles dig tunnels deep into subsoil.

A tortoise may sleep through winter in subsoil.

Toads hunt insects on the soil's surface.

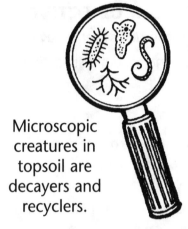

Microscopic creatures in topsoil are decayers and recyclers.

Roots grow down into subsoil.

Snails often hide in holes in topsoil.

Mother mole makes a nest for her babies deep in the subsoil.

Many insects lay eggs just below the soil's surface.

Some ants store seeds in their nests.

Robins feed on worms that live in topsoil.

Mushrooms help break down and recycle dead plants and animals in the topsoil.

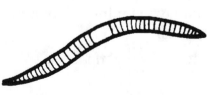

Dandelions grow one main root down into topsoil, from which side roots branch.

Earthworms loosen and mix topsoil as they tunnel through it.

Some beetles tunnel through topsoil.

# Caves

## Inside a Cave

This model illustrates how a cave forms.

### SCIENCE CONCEPTS & OBJECTIVES

- Identify how weathering helps create caves
- Infer that dissolved minerals build stalactites and stalagmites

### VOCABULARY

**calcite** calcium carbonate, the main ingredient of chalk and many sea- and eggshells, and the main mineral in limestone

**stalactite** an icicle-shaped calcite deposit hanging from the roof of a cave

**stalagmite** a cone-shaped calcite deposit built up on the floor of a cave

# For Your Information

As rainwater moves through air and soil, it picks up carbon dioxide. This turns the water into carbonic acid, a weak acid like soda water. When this acid seeps into cracks in limestone, it dissolves the mineral calcite and enlarges the cracks. Over time, this chemical weathering eats away holes in the underground limestone. Eventually the holes can grow into a cave. The calcite dissolved in water drips onto the cave's ceilings and floors. As the water evaporates, *stalactites* and *stalagmites* form.

Weathering is just the breaking down of rock. The process of rock being carried away and/or deposited elsewhere is actually erosion (see page 89). Therefore, strictly speaking, caves are made through a combination of weathering (breakdown of rock by dissolving calcite) and erosion (the removal and redeposit of the calcite somewhere else).

## TEACHING WITH THE MODEL

# Inside a Cave

1. Ask students: Has anyone ever seen the inside of a cave? (TV counts, too.) What was it like? What do you think weathering has to do with caves?

2. Invite students to make the model (see page 75).

3. Explain that the model represents a cross section through underground limestone.

*(continued on page 76)*

# Making the Model ✂

## Inside a Cave

**MATERIALS:** reproducible pages 79 and 80 ◎ crayons, colored pencils, or markers ◎ scissors ◎ glue or tape ◎ 9-by-12-inch construction paper or light cardboard ◎ blue ribbon or yarn (optional)

1. Photocopy pages 79 and 80.

2. Color the limestone on page 79 gray and the cracks in the limestone blue. Research authentic cave colors and color the cave scene on page 80.

3. Cut the rectangle out of page 79 along the heavy black outer lines.

4. Cut along the heavy black lines on the limestone rock to free the six flaps.

5. Turn the page over and bend back the flaps. Crease them along the dashed lines. Then flatten the flaps again.

6. Glue or tape the cave scene to a piece of construction paper or light cardboard. Make sure it's centered on the paper, as shown.

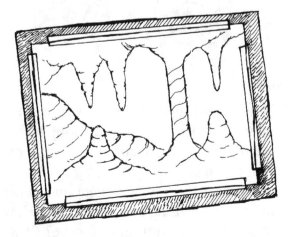

7. Turn the cave scene over so it's facedown. Line up the limestone page with the back of the cave scene and tape the two pieces together, as shown.

8. Turn both pieces over. Place a piece of tape on the untaped edge of the limestone rock page. Bring the limestone rock page together with the edge of the construction paper and tape. Then tape the corners.

9. Optional: Cut a small hole in an 8-by-5-inch piece of dark construction paper. Place it on top of the model. Lower a piece of blue ribbon or yarn through the hole and down into the cave. Tape the other end to the paper lid. The ribbon or yarn represents a river that feeds water into the cave from the surface. It is the source of the cave's underground river.

*(continued from page 74)*

4. Point out the cracks in the limestone on the outside of the model. Explain that water from rain, melted snow, or flooded rivers becomes a weak acid as it soaks into the ground. When this acid fills the cracks in limestone, it dissolves calcite—the main mineral in limestone—little by little and carries it away. Over time, the small cracks grow larger and larger until they join to form large holes. Invite students to push in the flaps on the model to create holes.

5. Ask students to look into the flaps and describe what the inside of the cave looks like.

6. Ask: What do you think is dripping from the cracks in the cave ceiling? Explain that it is the weak acid carrying the dissolved calcite. In the air of the open cave, some drops evaporate (change from a liquid into a gas) and leave behind a tiny bit of the mineral calcite on the ceiling. As the mineral hardens and additional drops leave more calcite on the ceiling, rock icicles called stalactites grow down from the ceiling.

7. Evaporation also takes place on the cave floor. There drops leave calcite that hardens and builds up into stalagmites. Challenge students to find a stalactite and a stalagmite in the model. Can they also point out places where a stalactite and a stalagmite may one day meet to form a column?

## EXTENSIONS

### HANDS-ON
# Cave in a Cup

**Students observe how chemical and mechanical weathering and erosion form caves.**

**MATERIALS:** sand ◉ tall, clear plastic cup ◉ sugar cubes ◉ wood glue ◉ nail ◉ deep bowl ◉ measuring cup ◉ warm water

1. Pour an inch of sand into the bottom of the cup.

2. Place a layer of sugar cubes on top of the sand. Then squirt wood glue over the cubes. Use enough glue so that it seeps down between the cubes.

3. Keep adding layers of sugar cubes topped with glue until the cup is nearly full. Let this "rock" dry overnight.

4. The next day, top the rock off with a layer of sand. Then poke a hole in the cup's bottom with the nail. Set the cup in a deep bowl.

5. Slowly pour several cups of warm water over the "rock." Ask: What happens? *(The water dissolves the sugar, leaving gaps and spaces between the hardened glue. The water also carries the dissolved sugar and sand out to the bowl, leaving crevices behind.)* How is this like the formation of a cave? *(Water seeps through rock, dissolves minerals, and deposits them elsewhere.)*

## HANDS-ON
# Stalactite or Stalagmite?

**Students create stalactites and stalagmites.**

MATERIALS: 2 glasses ◉ water ◉ Epsom salts ◉ spoon ◉ cotton yarn or string ◉ yardstick ◉ large paper clips ◉ pennies ◉ plate

1. Fill each glass with hot water. (If possible, heat the water on a stove or in a microwave.) Stir in Epsom salts until no more will dissolve.

2. Cut a piece of cotton yarn or string about 30 inches long. Fold it in half and twist the halves together. Tie a large paper clip to each end. Slide a penny into each paper clip for extra weight.

3. Dip the yarn in the Epsom salt solution to wet it thoroughly. Then place one end of the string in each glass.

4. Place the plate between the two glasses. Move the glasses apart until string hangs an inch or two above the plate, in a deep U shape, as shown.

5. Check the setup daily for four to five days and keep a log of their observations. After deposits begin to accumulate on and under the string, ask: What do you see forming? *(Epsom salt crystals)* Where did they come from? *(the solution in the glasses)* How are the formations like stalactites and stalagmites? *(The yarn acts like a wick, drawing up the water and dissolved salts. This solution*

*then drips off the yarn. As the water evaporates, the salts recrystalize on the string and on the plate, just as stalactites and stalagmites form on the ceiling and floor of a cave.)*

## COOPERATE AND CREATE
# Cave Quest

**Students find out about other kinds of caves.**

Divide students into groups and assign each group a type of cave (lava cave, sea cave, ice cave, or coral cave). Invite them to research their cave type, finding out where it occurs, how it's formed, and how common it is. Then challenge them to create a diorama of their type of cave similar to the model.

## RESEARCH IT

Related topics for research reports or projects:
- How did a cowboy discover Carlsbad Caverns in 1902?
- What kinds of animals live in caves? Do any plants live in them?
- Are there any caves in your state? If so, where?

# WEATHERING RESOURCES

## BOOKS FOR STUDENTS

*Caves and Caverns* by Gail Gibbons (Harcourt Brace, 1993)

*One Small Square: Backyard* and *Cave* by Donald M. Silver and Patricia J. Wynne (McGraw-Hill, 1997)

*Soil* by Karen Bryant-Mole (Raintree Steck-Vaughn, 1996)

*Underground Life* by Allan Roberts (Children's Press, 1983)

## BOOKS FOR TEACHERS

*Chiseling the Earth: How Erosion Shapes the Land* by R. V. Fodor (Enslow, 1983)

*Earth: The Ever Changing Planet* by Donald M. Silver (Random House, 1989)

*Earth Science Activities for Grades 2–8* by Marvin N. Tolman and James O. Morton (Prentice Hall, 1986)

## OTHER RESOURCES

*Ask-a-geologist* Geologists at the U.S. Geological Survey are available on-line to answer students' earth science questions (E-mail: usgs.gov).

*Geology: Weathering and Erosion* Mac/Windows CD-ROM (National Geographic Educational Technology, 1994)

*The National Speleological Society* 2813 Cave Avenue, Huntsville, AL 35810-4431 (E-mail: http://www.caves.org/~nss). Write or E-mail this organization to find out about caves near you.

*One Small Square: Backyard* Mac/Windows CD-ROM (Virgin Sound and Vision, 1995)

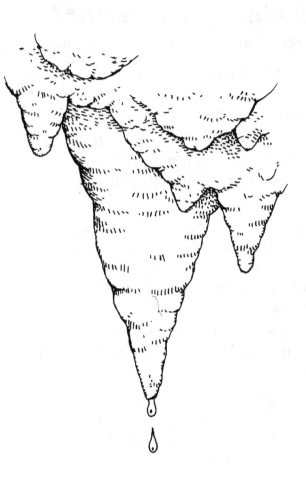

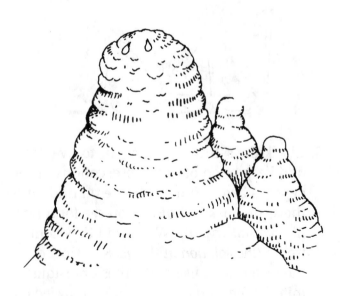

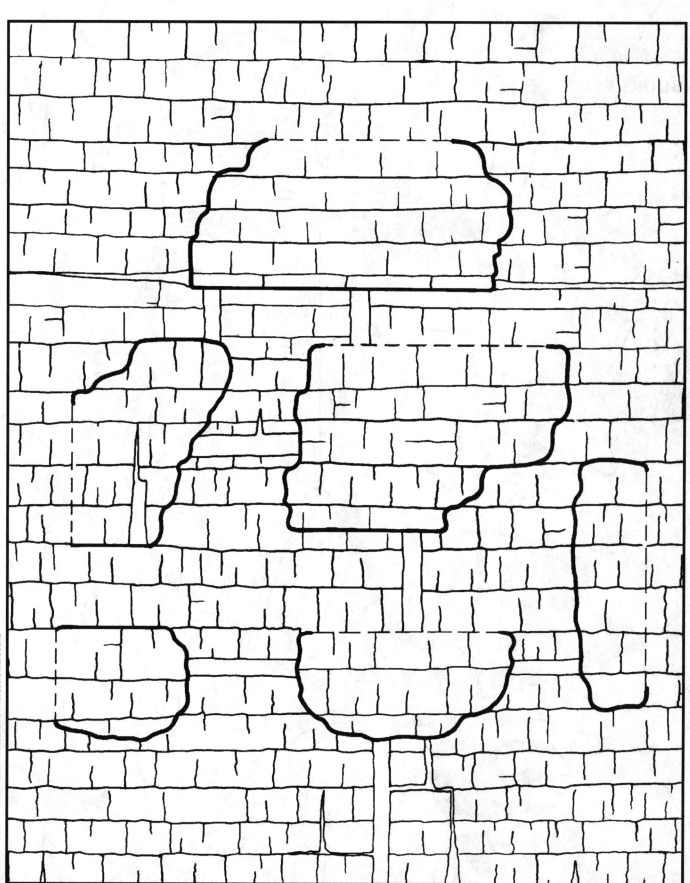

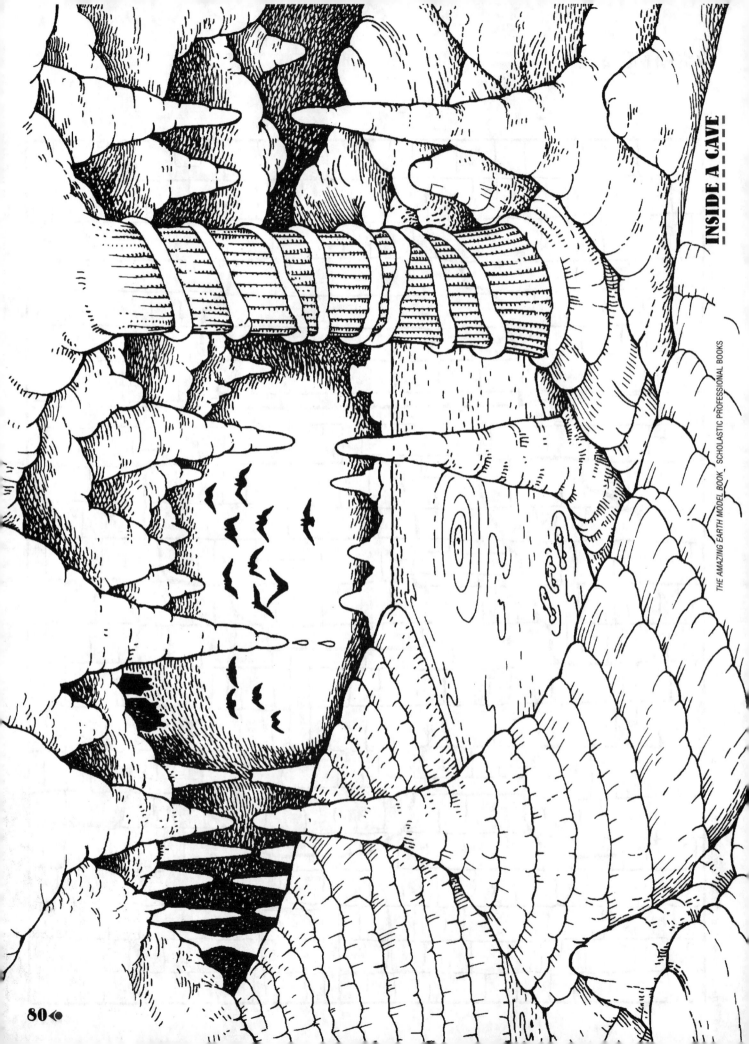

THE AMAZING EARTH MODEL BOOK _ SCHOLASTIC PROFESSIONAL BOOKS

# Water Cycle

## Water-go-Round

This model illustrates the water cycle.

### SCIENCE CONCEPTS & OBJECTIVES

⟐ Infer how the water cycle works

⟐ Understand the difference between evaporation and condensation

### VOCABULARY

**condensation**  the process by which water vapor (a gas) changes to liquid water

**evaporation**  the process by which liquid water changes to water vapor (a gas)

**water cycle**  the cycle of evaporation, condensation, precipitation, and runoff that determines water movement between the land, oceans, and atmosphere

## For Your Information

Water covers most of Earth's surface and also helps shape the land. The water that flows in rivers carves out canyons and V-shaped valleys. As glacier ice, water scrapes and scours mountains. Water also carries tons of sediment to the sea, where sedimentary rocks will form future land. Water is part of every kind of plant and animal and makes life on our planet possible.

When water warms and evaporates, it enters the air as water vapor, a gas. When water vapor cools and condenses, it turns into tiny droplets that form clouds. The water droplets in clouds then fall as raindrops upon further cooling. All the ways water moves from the ocean, to the air, to the land, and back again make up the water cycle.

## TEACHING WITH THE MODEL

## Water-go-Round

1. Ask students: Where is most of the water on Earth? *(In the ocean; it holds 97 percent of Earth's water.)* Why doesn't the supply of water run out? *(Earth's water supply replenishes itself through the water cycle.)*

2. Invite students to make and color the model (see page 82).

3. Challenge students to flip their books from back to front and figure out the path of water as it moves in a cycle from the ocean, to the air, to the land, and back to the ocean. Ask students what they think is happening to the water in the ocean at the

# Making the Model

## Water-go-Round

**MATERIALS:** reproducible page 84 ⊙ crayons, colored pencils, or markers

1. Photocopy page 84. TIP: To make a sturdier book, first paste the page to another sheet of paper and let it dry.

2. Color the 16 pictures, if desired.

3. Cut out the 16 pictures along the solid black lines.

4. Stack the pictures in order with number 1 on top and number 16 on the bottom.

5. Line up the book's pages so the edges at the right-hand side are as even as possible. Then staple on the left-hand side, as shown.

start of the flip book. *(Heat from the sun causes the water to evaporate and enter the air as a gas, called water vapor.)*

4. Then ask: What forms at the top of the arrows? *(a cloud)* Why? *(As water vapor cools, it changes from a gas to tiny drops of water that form clouds. This process is called condensation.)*

5. Where does the cloud move in the flip book? *(over the land)* What happens there? *(As they cool further, the droplets in the cloud get larger and larger until they fall as rain.)*

6. What happens to the water that falls as rain? *(It runs off the land into streams that join with the rivers that carry the water back to the ocean.)*

7. What happens to the water in the ocean? *(Some of it evaporates into the air.)* Have students flip their books again and again to emphasize that the water cycle never ends.

8. Challenge students to identify where else water evaporates from besides the ocean. *(lakes, rivers, trees)* Then invite them to create their own flip books that illustrate the water cycle.

## EXTENSIONS

### HANDS-ON
# Water Cycler

**Students create and observe a mini–water cycle.**

**MATERIALS:** clear plastic box with a clear lid ⊙ small bowl ⊙ water ⊙ lamp ⊙ ice cubes ⊙ plastic bag that zips closed

1. Set the bowl in the box at one end. Fill it with water. This is your "ocean." Close the lid.

2. Position the lamp a few inches over the box's lid, directly over the bowl of water. The lamp is the "sun."

3. Turn the "sun" on and let it shine over the "ocean" for two hours. After two hours, ask: What happened? *(Water in the bowl evaporated.)* Where is the water? *(It's in the air inside of the box in the form of water vapor, and some condensed into drops inside the lid.)*

4. Now put ice cubes in the plastic bag and zip it closed. Set the bag of ice on top of the lid at the opposite end of the box from the lamp. Leave the lamp on and wait another two hours. Ask: What happened? *(It rained.)* Why? *(The ice cooled the temperature inside the box, and the water vapor condensed into droplets that fell as rain.)*

## COOPERATE AND CREATE
# Water Dependent

**Student groups investigate their local source of water and present ideas for conserving water.**

Explain to students that although water covers more than 70 percent of Earth's surface, only 1 percent is fit for consumption. (Ninety-seven percent is salt water and the other 2 percent is fresh water trapped in glacier ice.) Over half of that 1 percent is inaccessible, far beneath Earth's surface. Although the amount of water on Earth always remains the same, a growing population has increased demands on the available water supply. In addition, pollution has made several water sources unusable.

Have the class find out where their fresh water comes from and how much of a supply is stored (a week's worth, a month's worth). When students comprehend the need to use water wisely, challenge groups to come up with ideas to promote water conservation. They can present their ideas as advertising campaigns. Invite them to create an ad poster or write and act out a TV or radio ad.

## RESEARCH IT

Related topics for research reports or projects:
- Where is Earth's water held? What percentage is in the oceans, rivers, lakes, or as ice?
- What are the different kinds of precipitation?
- How might global warming affect the water cycle and sea levels?

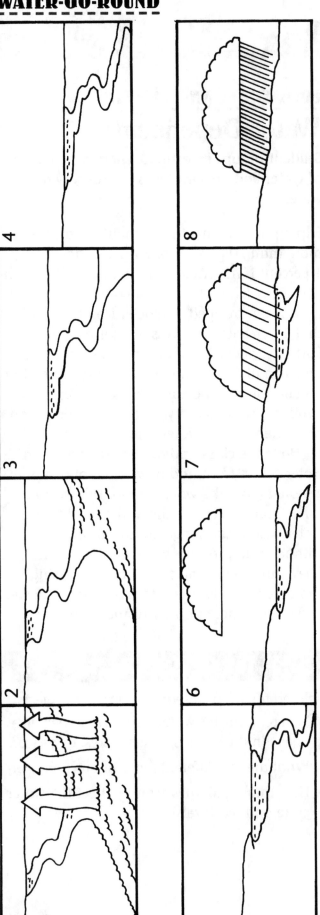

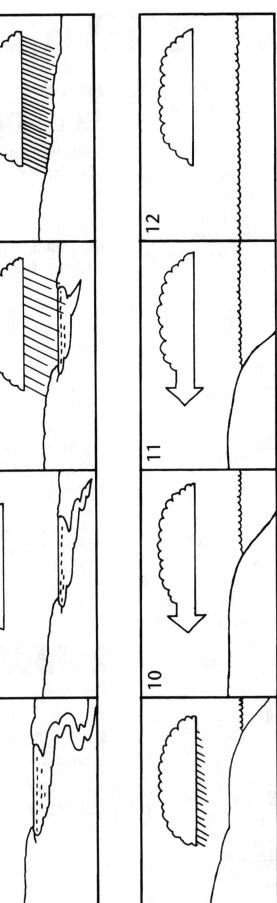

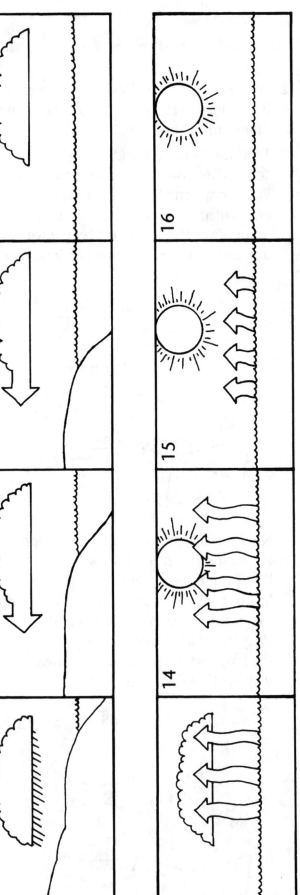

THE AMAZING EARTH MODEL BOOK   SCHOLASTIC PROFESSIONAL BOOKS

# A Geyser Erupts

## Gushing Geyser

This model shows how a geyser works.

### SCIENCE CONCEPTS & OBJECTIVES

◗ Understand why a geyser erupts

◗ Infer that water shot out of geysers can deposit minerals on land

### VOCABULARY

**geyser**  steam and very hot water that erupt from cracks in Earth's crust

**groundwater**  all the water that collects underground

## For Your Information

A geyser is an eruption of a column of steam and very hot water out of the ground. The eruption can last from seconds to an hour and happen every few minutes to every several years. Old Faithful, the famous geyser in Yellowstone National Park, erupts about every 70 minutes and shoots steam and hot water 12 stories into the air. The eruption is caused by chambers of superheated water underground. When the water boils and enough pressure builds up, water and steam are forced up and go shooting into the air above ground.

The water that shoots out of a geyser is groundwater. It fills hollow underground chambers and is superheated by hot igneous rocks. Nearly all groundwater comes from rain and melted snow that seep into soil and move

down to fill the cracks and spaces in and between rocks.

## TEACHING WITH THE MODEL

## Gushing Geyser

1. Ask students: What is a geyser? *(steam and hot water from underground that erupt into the air)* Where does the water come from? *(It's groundwater that comes from rain and melted snow that seep into the ground.)*

2. Invite students to make the model (see page 86).

3. Ask students to pull down on the bottom tab of their models. Explain that they are looking at a cross section of the inside of a

# Making the Model ✂

## Gushing Geyser

**MATERIALS:** reproducible page 88 ◎ scissors ◎ crayons, markers, or colored pencils

1. Photocopy page 88.

2. Cut out the two large pieces along their heavy black outer lines.

3. Cut out the two spaces labeled CUT OUT on the rectangular piece and discard them.

4. Cut open the two slits on the rectangular piece along their heavy black lines.

5. Color the areas labeled WATER and HEATING WATER CHAMBER blue. Color the HOT IGNEOUS ROCKS red. Color the remaining parts of the model, if desired.

6. Insert the smaller piece into the back of the rectangular piece as shown.

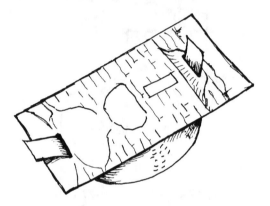

7. Pull the BOTTOM tab down to begin.

---

geyser. Point out the chamber that fills with groundwater.

4. Ask: What heats the water in the chamber? Explain that hot igneous rocks superheat the water, causing it to expand and push out of the chamber. The instant it does, the pressure releases and some of the water boils, creating steam.

5. Ask: As the water boils to steam, what happens? *(It expands.)* What can this cause? *(a geyser to erupt)* Invite students to find out for themselves by pulling up on the top tab. Explain that steam surges to the surface, forcing water out the top with it. The geyser shoots steam and hot water into the air for a minute or more.

6. Point out the emptying chamber in the model. Ask: What will happen when the chamber completely empties? *(The eruption will stop.)* Ask: When will an eruption happen again? *(when the chamber has refilled and heated again)* Allow students to pull down on the bottom tab to repeat the process.

7. Point out the hardened mound of minerals built up around the geyser's opening. Ask: How did it get there? Explain that underground water dissolves and carries minerals. When super-hot water shoots out of the geyser and cools, it evaporates, leaving behind tiny bits of minerals that harden. These minerals can build up into a mound over time.

# EXTENSIONS

## HANDS-ON
# Drop by Drop

Students observe how water that contains dissolved minerals can leave deposits when the water evaporates.

MATERIALS: cup of water ⊙ salt ⊙ measuring spoons ⊙ eyedropper or straw ⊙ flat dish

1. Add about two tablespoons of salt to the cup of water. Stir well until dissolved.

2. Fill the dropper or straw with the salty water. Drop ten drops on the dish, spacing them apart.

3. Let the dish sit until the water evaporates. Allow students to observe what is left behind on the dish. Ask: What is it? *(salt)* Where did it come from? *(It was dissolved in the water.)* What would happen if more drops kept depositing more salt in the same spots? *(A mound could develop.)*

## COOPERATE AND CREATE
# More Hot Water

Student groups investigate various results of water that is heated undergound.

Geysers are just one product of superheated groundwater. Challenge student groups to find out about others, including sulfur-mud pools (also called mud pots or paint pots), hot springs, and fumaroles. Students can make diagrams of how each works, or create a model similar to the geyser model.

# RESEARCH IT

Related topics for research reports or projects:

◗ What is the water table?

◗ Most of the world's geysers are in Iceland, New Zealand, or the western United States. What do these places have in common?

◗ What is geothermal energy?

# GUSHING GEYSER

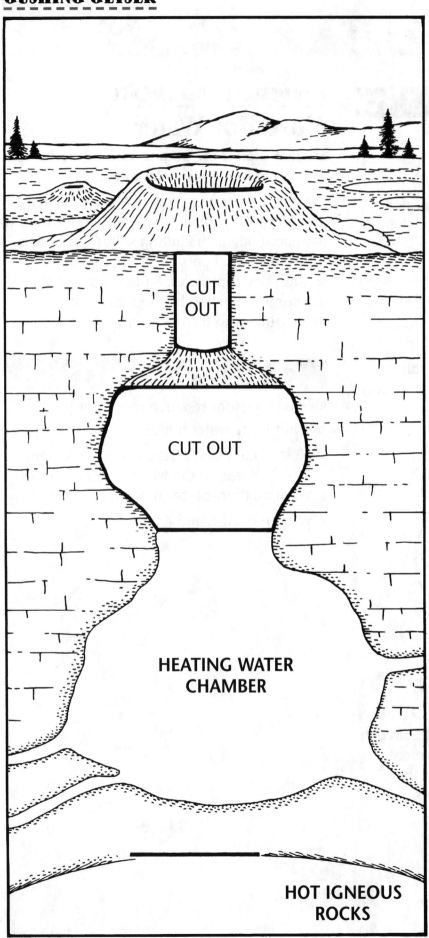

CUT
OUT

CUT OUT

HEATING WATER
CHAMBER

HOT IGNEOUS
ROCKS

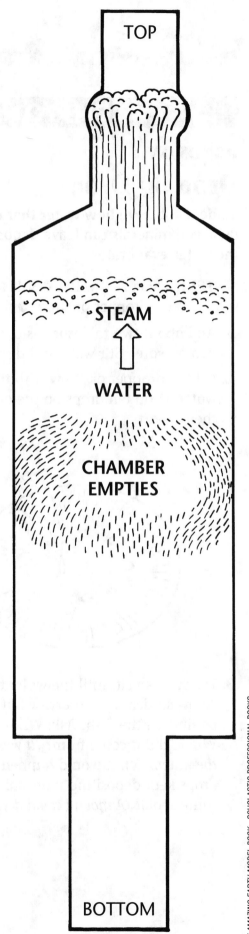

TOP

STEAM

WATER

CHAMBER
EMPTIES

BOTTOM

THE AMAZING EARTH MODEL BOOK    SCHOLASTIC PROFESSIONAL BOOKS

# Erosion

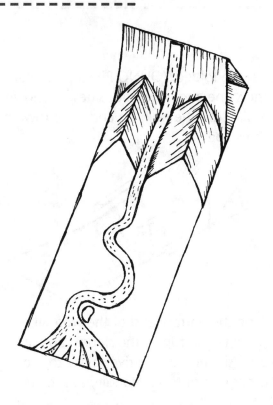

## A River's Run

This model shows the stages in the life of a river.

### SCIENCE CONCEPTS & OBJECTIVES

◈ Understand the effects of erosion

◈ Infer how rivers shape the land

### VOCABULARY

**bed**  the part of the land covered by a river or stream

**erosion**  the process of picking up and carrying away sediment from one place and depositing it in another

## For Your Information

Erosion is the process of picking up, carrying away, and depositing sediment. Whenever it rains, water washes over the land, picking up loose soil and weathered rocks and carrying them away. This runoff carves gullies as it washes into streams. Those streams join together and eventually form rivers.

Gravity pulls the water in rivers and streams downhill. Silt and other small sediments move along, suspended in the water. However, pebbles and larger sediments roll and tumble along a river's bed, rubbing and grinding away like cutting tools. When a river is young, it rapidly flows downhill in a fairly straight line, its sediment carving out a narrow V-shaped valley. As a river matures, its slower-moving sediments cut more from side to side and create winding S-shaped loops.

## TEACHING WITH THE MODEL

## A River's Run

1. Ask students: What do you know about rivers? Is the water fresh or salty? *(fresh)* Where does the water in rivers come from? *(rain and melting snow)* Is the water moving or still? *(moving)*

2. Invite students to make the model (see page 90).

3. Challenge students to describe the river on their models. Have them point to the different parts and explain how they are alike or different. The parts and stages of a river are highlighted in Life of a River (see page 91).

# Making the Model ✂

## A River's Run

**MATERIALS:** reproducible page 93 ◎ scissors ◎ tape ◎ crayons or markers ◎ glue (optional)

1. Photocopy page 93.

2. Cut out the four pieces. Color them, if desired.

3. Fold the small square piece along its dashed line so the printed side is up, as shown.

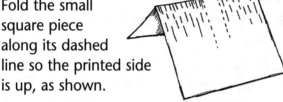

4. Set this folded piece on top of the long rectangular piece and tape, as shown. Make sure the folded piece lines up with the dotted line and that the edges are even. The piece should form a gentle slope.

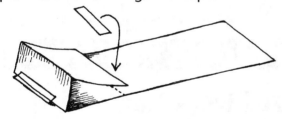

5. Fold the piece labeled YOUNG RIVER accordion style, as shown.

6. Set the folded YOUNG RIVER piece next to the slope and tape both sides, as shown. Make sure the pointed ends face toward the slope.

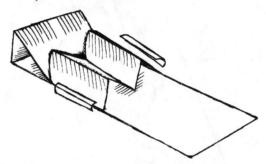

7. Tape the narrow end of the wormlike river piece to the top of the slope. Tape the opposite end of the river piece to the other end of the rectangle, as shown.

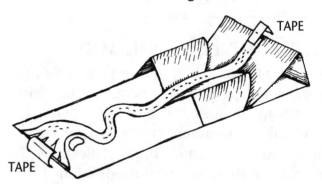

TAPE

TAPE

8. Tack down the river with tape or glue if it bulges up.

4. Review the stages of a river and ask: In which stage does the river cut through mountains? *(young river)* In which stage is there an oxbow lake? *(old river)* How does the landscape change from the mountains to the sea? *(flat-tens)* Why do you think this area floods during times of heavy rains and melting snow? *(The floodplain is level with the river. Excess water spills over onto the land.)* Are there rivers in our state that flood?

# Life of a River

- Rivers change as they age. *Young rivers* flow rapidly downhill in a straight line. The sediments they carry cut deeply into the rocks below, eroding them and carving out a narrow *V-shaped valley.*

- A *mature river* flows more slowly along the bottom of the valley it carved out when young. Over time, the steep sides of the valley are worn down by weathering. No longer does the river cut down into rock. Instead, cutting takes place from side to side, creating winding S-shaped loops. This process flattens and widens the valley floor. The area a mature river covers with flood-water is its *floodplain.*

- An *old river* flows slowly over its broad floodplain. The walls of its valley are worn down. In places its wide loops join, and the river takes a shortcut through the join-ing loop ends. When mud and silt separate the cutoff loop ends from the rest of the river, an *oxbow lake* forms.

- A river slows down when it enters the sea and deposits the sediment it carries. Where the sea is quiet, the sediment sinks to the seafloor and piles up into a fan-shaped *delta* that can rise out of the water, forming new land.

## EXTENSIONS

### HANDS-ON
# Slowly Disappearing
**Students observe the earth-moving power of erosion.**

**MATERIALS:** 2 pans ◉ soil ◉ watering can ◉ water ◉ book or piece of wood

NOTE: Do this activity outside, in a large tub, or on plastic or newspaper.

1. Completely fill the pans with packed soil.

2. Make furrows across the width of one of the pans.

3. Raise one end of both pans and set the ends on a book or piece of wood so they slope downward. Make sure the furrowed pan's furrows run horizontally.

4. Gently sprinkle water from the watering can over both of the pans' raised ends. Make sure each receives an equal amount of water. Ask: What happens? *(The water picks up and carries away the soil—it erodes the soil.)* In which pan does less erosion occur? Why? *(In the pan with soil furrows. The furrows catch and hold water, like terraces in fields.)*

## COOPERATE AND CREATE
# Old Man River

**Students investigate the stages and features of well-known rivers.**

Challenge student groups to find out more about rivers they are familiar with, such as the Colorado, Missouri, Mississippi, Amazon, Nile, or a local river. Have them create a poster that maps out the river's path with labeled parts, using the model as a guide.

## RESEARCH IT

Related topics for research reports or projects:

- Which U.S. rivers have experienced major floods in recent years? What have been the effects of these floods?

- How did Niagara Falls form?

- How do ocean waves erode beaches and shores?

- What was the Dust Bowl of the 1930s?

- What is soil conservation?

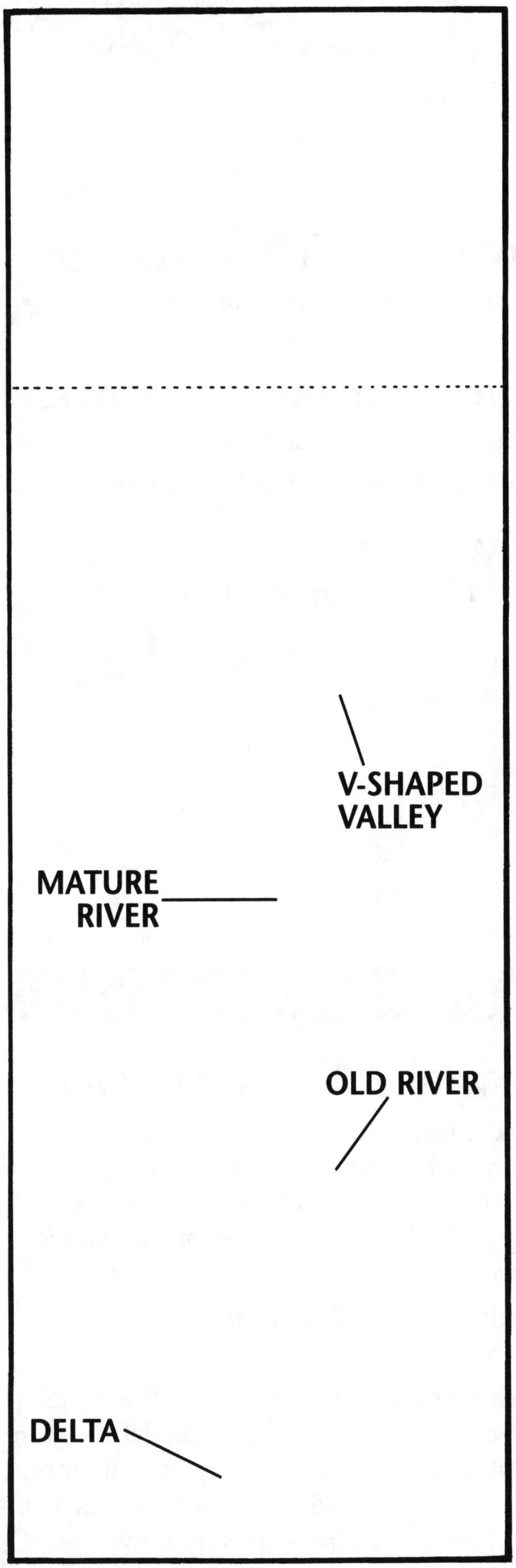

V-SHAPED
VALLEY

MATURE
RIVER

OLD RIVER

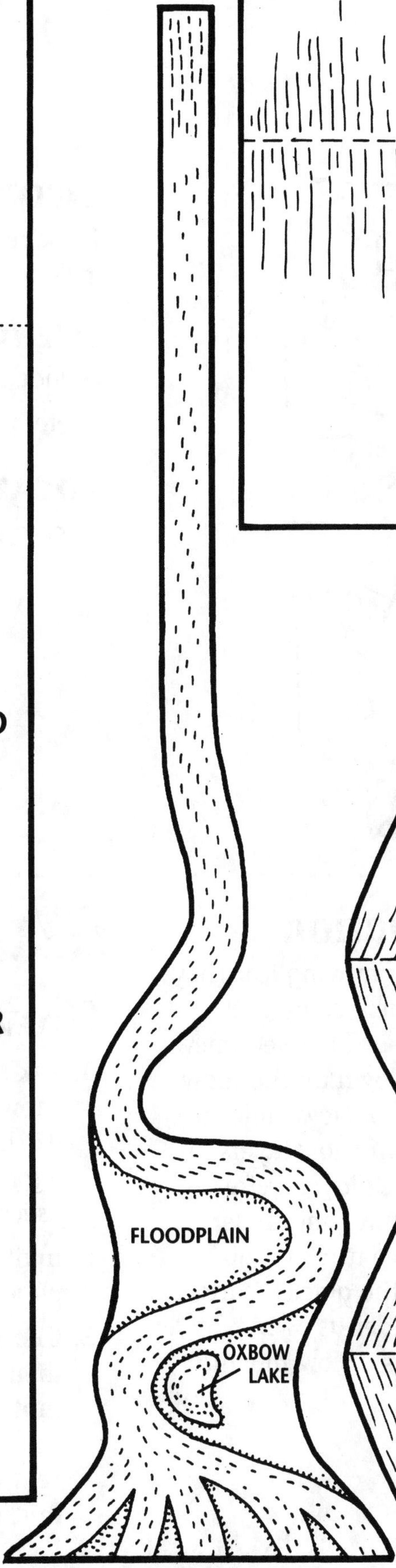

FLOODPLAIN

OXBOW
LAKE

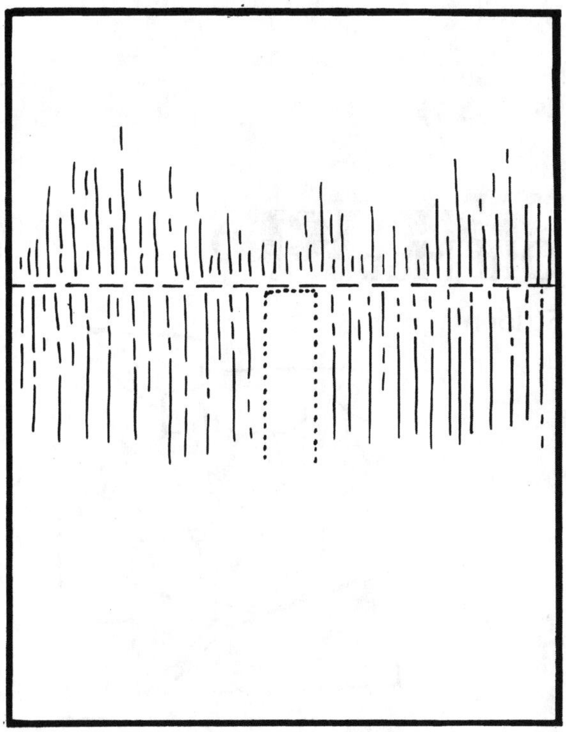

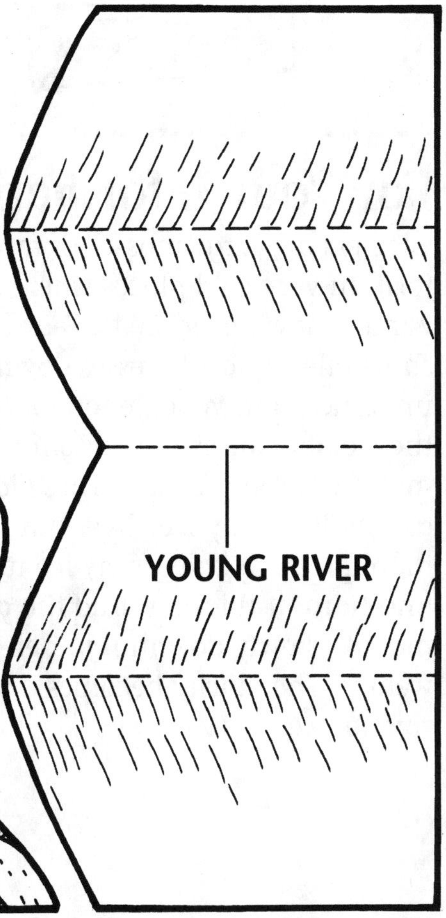

YOUNG RIVER

DELTA

THE AMAZING EARTH MODEL BOOK   SCHOLASTIC PROFESSIONAL BOOKS

# Glaciers

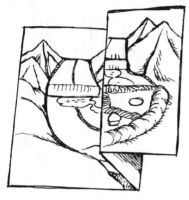

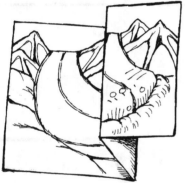

## Grow and Melt a Glacier

These models show glaciers forming and melting.

### SCIENCE CONCEPTS & OBJECTIVES

→Understand what a glacier is and how it forms

→Infer that glaciers are agents of erosion

### VOCABULARY

**glacier**  a slow-moving river of ice

## For Your Information

Glaciers are large masses of moving ice. They form in very cold places where some of the winter snow never melts. Year after year, new snow piles up and presses down on the snow underneath it. When enough snow builds up, the weight causes the bottom snow layers to melt from the pressure. These layers refreeze as rough, grainy ice. Over time and under more pressure, the grainy ice turns rough and hard. It thickens, and the glacier starts moving slowly downhill under its own weight. The glacier becomes a slow-moving river of ice.

## TEACHING WITH THE MODEL

## Grow and Melt a Glacier

1. Ask students: Have you ever made a snowball? What happens if you hard-pack it? *(It turns icy.)* Why? *(The pressure of packing melts the outermost layer and it refreezes as ice.)*

2. Invite students to make the models (see page 95) and color them.

3. Challenge students to describe the scene on their folded Grow a Glacier model. Explain that a glacier formed on top of a mountain where all of the winter snow never melted. Year after year, the unmelted snow thickened and new snow squeezed and

# Making the Model ✂

## Grow and Melt a Glacier

**MATERIALS:** reproducible pages 98 and 99 ◉ scissors ◉ crayons, markers, or colored pencils

1. Photocopy pages 98 and 99. Color the model, if desired.

2. Cut the Grow a Glacier model out of page 98 along its solid black outer line.

3. Fold the model along the dashed line that's nearly in the center so the printed sides are on the inside. Crease well and reopen.

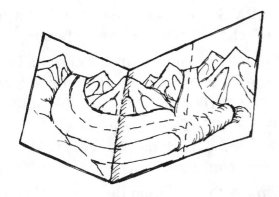

4. Fold the other dashed line of the model so the far right flap goes back, the printed side on the outside. Crease well.

5. The finished, closed model should appear as shown.

6. Repeat steps 2 to 5 for the Melt a Glacier model on page 99.

pressed it. When the thick, unmelted snow turned to ice, it became so heavy that it started to move downhill under its own weight as a glacier.

4. Ask students to open their model and describe what they see. Here are some things to point out:

◈ **Rocks frozen inside the glacier.** These rocks were pried loose by the glacier as it moved. They act as cutting tools, eroding the land. Ask: Where did the big rocks on top of the glacier come from? (*The glacier carried them there.*)

◈ **Deep bowl-shaped basins and sharp jagged ridges on mountaintops carved out by the glaciers.** Ask: What happened to the shape of the valley? (*As the glacier moved down the valley, it ground away the*

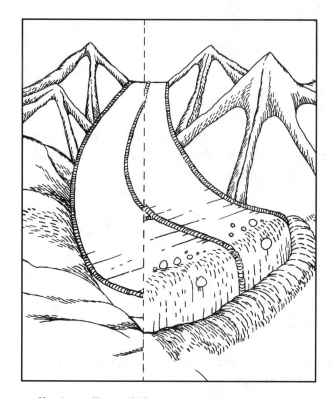

*valley's walls and floor and changed it from a deep V-shaped valley to a U-shaped valley.)*

● **Crevasses or cracks in the glacier.** They can be 100 feet (30 meters) deep.

● **The terminal moraine** is the mound of debris pushed along the front of the glacier. The debris can range in size from dust-sized particles to boulders.

5. Challenge students to predict what will happen when the leading edge of the glacier moves to a warmer place and starts melting. Ask them to describe the picture on their folded Melt a Glacier model, then unfold it and describe how the glacier alters the landscape when it melts. Explain that the rocks that were trapped in the ice have been deposited and built up ridges, hills, and mounds. Impress upon students that the front end of a glacier may stay in one place for a time. In that case, the bottom, flowing ice will keep delivering rocks to the melting edge.

6. The Melt a Glacier model illustrates many unique land formations created by alpine glaciers, including drumlins, erratics, glacial lakes, kames, eskers, tarns, hanging valleys, waterfalls, and U-shaped valleys. Challenge students to find out what these formations are and how the glacier formed them.

## EXTENSIONS

### HANDS-ON
# Scouring Ice

**Students investigate how ice with embedded sediment can wear away surfaces.**

MATERIALS: ice cubes ◉ sand ◉ dish ◉ newspaper ◉ chalk ◉ rubber gloves ◉ freezer

1. Place the ice cubes in a dish of sand. Let them stand at room temperature for 5 to 6 minutes. Then put the entire dish in the freezer overnight.

2. Give groups of students stacks of old newspaper, chalk, and gloves.

3. Remove the dish from the freezer. If necessary, separate the cubes using a towel or glove.

4. Quickly hand out a cube to each student. Using a gloved hand, have students rub the cube, sand side down, over the newspaper stack and over the pieces of chalk. Ask: What happens? *(The ice tears up the newspaper and wears away the chalk, leaving bits of sand behind.)* How is this like what a glacier can do? *(Glaciers can wear away rock and move and deposit soil.)*

## COOPERATE AND CREATE
# Glacier Detectives

**Students learn about the two main kinds of glaciers.**

Challenge student groups to find out about one of the main types of glaciers: alpine or continental. How and where are they formed? How do they change the land? Invite students to build dioramas to illustrate their type of glacier's features.

## RESEARCH IT

Related topics for research reports or papers:

● How fast (or slowly) do glaciers move?

● When was the last Ice Age? Which parts of Earth were covered by glaciers?

● What are some famous examples of land formations left by glaciers? (Bunker Hill in Boston is a famous drumlin, for example.)

## WATER & EROSION RESOURCES

### BOOKS FOR STUDENTS

*Icebergs and Glaciers* by Seymour Simon (Morrow, 1987)

*Soil Erosion and Pollution* by Darlene R. Stille (Children's Press, 1990)

*Water Up, Water Down: The Hydrologic Cycle* by Sally M. Walker (Carolrhoda Books, 1992)

### BOOKS FOR TEACHERS

*Earth Science for Every Kid* by Janice VanCleave (Wiley, 1991)

*Great Rivers of the World* (National Geographic Society, 1984)

*Tapping Earth's Heat* by Patricia Lauber (Garrard, 1978)

### OTHER RESOURCES

*Explore Yellowstone* Mac/Windows CD-ROM (MECC/The Learning Co., 1996)

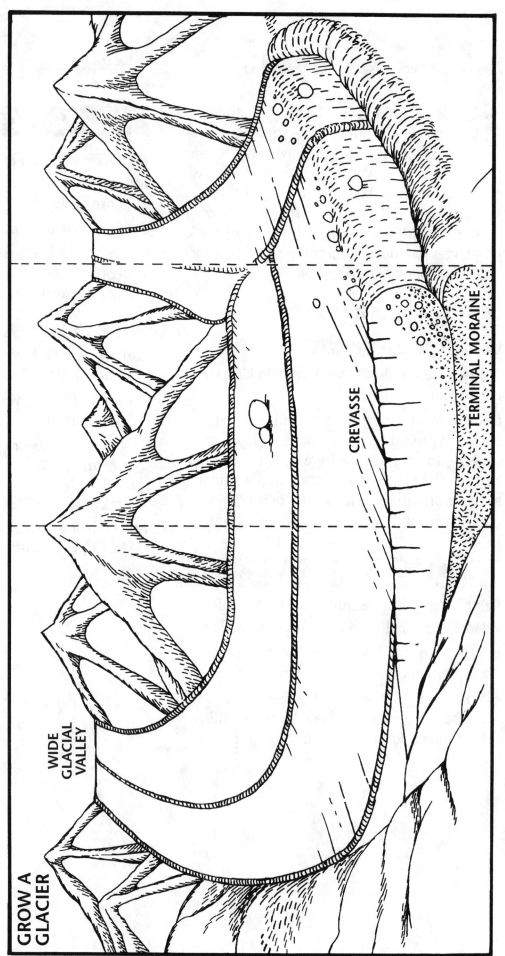

GROW A
GLACIER

WIDE
GLACIAL
VALLEY

CREVASSE

TERMINAL MORAINE

*THE AMAZING EARTH MODEL BOOK*   SCHOLASTIC PROFESSIONAL BOOKS

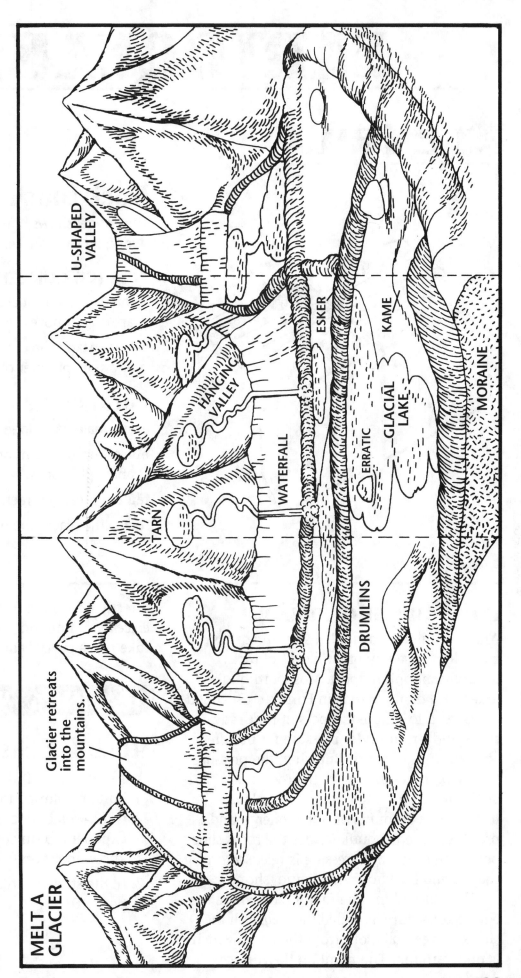

MELT A
GLACIER

Glacier retreats
into the
mountains.

U-SHAPED
VALLEY

HANGING
VALLEY

TARN

WATERFALL

ESKER

KAME

ERRATIC

GLACIAL
LAKE

DRUMLINS

MORAINE

# EARTHQUAKES

## At a Fault

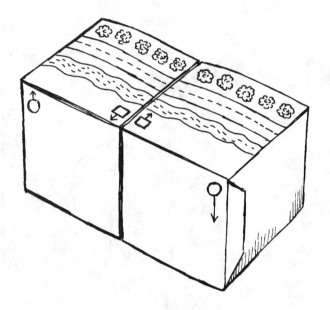

## Rock Blocks

This model shows how rocks move along faults during an earthquake.

### SCIENCE CONCEPTS & OBJECTIVES

- Infer that earthquakes occur when rock snaps apart and moves along a fault
- Understand the difference between the focus and the epicenter of an earthquake

### VOCABULARY

**earthquake**  a sudden shift in Earth's crust

**epicenter**  the point on Earth's surface directly above the focus

**fault**  a break, or fracture on Earth's crust

**focus**  the place where an earthquake begins

---

## For Your Information

An earthquake is a sudden shift in Earth's crust. It's caused by great blocks of rocks abruptly snapping apart. Most earthquakes take place along breaks in Earth's crust called *faults*. At a fault, great blocks of rock may stress and strain under pressure for hundreds or thousands of years. But when the pressure finally becomes too great, the rock blocks suddenly move past each other. This releases tremendous amounts of stored energy and produces an earthquake. After the rocks slide past each other, the pressure is released and they spring back to their original shape.

The place along the fault break where the earthquake starts is called the *focus*. All the shock waves travel out from the focus, which is underground. The point on the surface directly above the focus is the earthquake's *epicenter*. More than a million earthquakes take place every year around the world.

## TEACHING WITH THE MODEL

## Rock Blocks

1. Ask students: If the ground beneath this building started to shake, what would you think was happening? Has anyone ever experienced an earthquake or do you know about one? What happened?

2. Invite students to make the model (see page 101).

*(continued on page 102)*

# Making the Model ✂

## Rock Blocks

**MATERIALS:** reproducible pages 104 and 105
◉ scissors ◉ tape ◉ crayons, markers, or colored pencils (optional)

1. Photocopy pages 104 and 105.

2. Cut out each page's piece along its heavy black line. Color each, if desired.

3. Select one of the pieces and fold all the dashed lines away from the printed side, as shown. Crease the folds well.

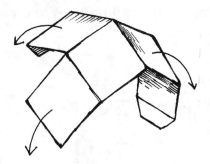

4. Fold the long strip of four squares upon itself to form a closed square and tape the tab, as shown.

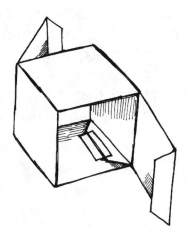

5. Fold in the tab of one of the remaining sides and tape from the inside, as shown.

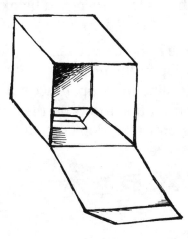

6. Close the final side with the tab on the outside and tape, as shown.

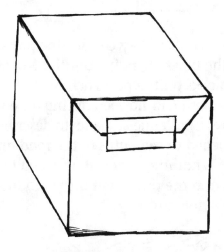

7. Repeat steps 3–6 for the other piece. HINT: Taping all the edges will reinforce and strengthen the cubes.

*(continued from page 100)*

3. Set the two assembled blocks side by side with their RIVER and ROAD printed sides facing up. Place them next to each other so that the tiny squares with arrows are side by side. Explain that students are looking down on trees, a road, and a river. Beneath this land there is a break in Earth's crust called a fault.

4. Place one hand on each block and push them in opposite directions as if you were going to slide them apart according to the directions of the arrows on the little squares. However, don't actually let the blocks move.

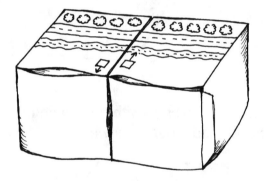

5. Ask students if they can see the pressure. Are the blocks bending a little? Now slide the blocks a little past each other. Such movement can happen during an earthquake. Challenge students to describe what happened to the paths of the road and the river. What might have happened to the trees and the pavement if the ground shook violently?

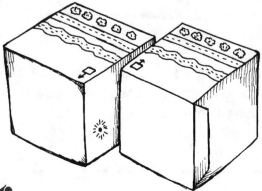

6. The movement of the blocks took place along a crack—a fault. Look for the FOCUS on the side of one of the moved blocks. The focus is the place where the earthquake began. The point on the surface directly above the focus is the epicenter.

7. During earthquakes, blocks of rocks can move up and down in relation to each other. Place the blocks next to each other so the circles with arrows are side by side.

8. Hold up the blocks and move them in the direction of the arrows. Challenge students to describe how the land changed from this upward movement. Point out the side of the upward-moving block. It shows a waterfall and falling trees and rocks.

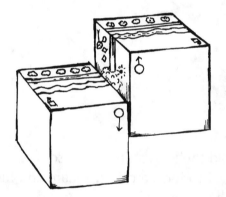

9. Challenge students to find the focus near the waterfall and to figure out where the epicenter is. Then explain that once the rocks slide past each other and release stored-up energy, they spring back to their original shape, helping to relieve the pressure.

## EXTENSIONS

### HANDS-ON
# Center Split

Students observe how vibrations can split rock along a fault line.

MATERIALS: rectangular block of modeling clay ○ knife ○ cookie sheet ○ sand or topsoil ○ wooden ruler

1. Set the block of clay on its long narrow side and cut the block in half at an angle. To do this, set the knife on top of the block perpendicular to it. Cut down through the block, angling to the left. This is the fault line in the "rock."

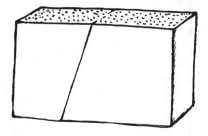

2. Pick up the two "rock" pieces together and set them toward one end of the cookie sheet. Sprinkle sand on top of the "rocks." This is the "ground."

3. Place the cookie sheet on the edge of a table. Pull the cookie sheet out so the beginning edge of the "fault" is just over the edge of the table. Adjust the "rocks" on the sheet until they balance.

4. Start tapping the ruler on the bottom of the cookie sheet, just underneath where the beginning edge of the "fault" is. Stop when a crack in the "ground" is apparent. Ask: What happened? *(The "rock" slipped apart along the fault and cracked open the ground.)* Why? *(vibrations)* How is this like an earth-

quake? *(The ground above a fault shifts when an earthquake produces vibrations.)*

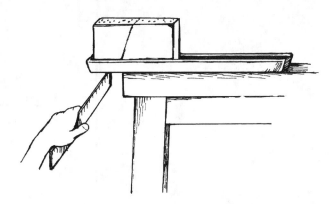

### COOPERATE AND CREATE
# Famous Fault

**Students research the San Andreas fault.**

The San Andreas fault runs for about a thousand miles through Southern California. Encourage students to find out more about this famous fault by challenging groups to draw a map of it, create a timeline of known quakes along it, or write futuristic stories of the "Big One" yet to come.

## RESEARCH IT

Related topics for research reports and projects:

◆ How were fault block mountains like the Sierra Nevadas in California and the Tetons in Wyoming formed?

◆ Where do most major earthquakes (those that cause damage) occur? What is the Richter scale?

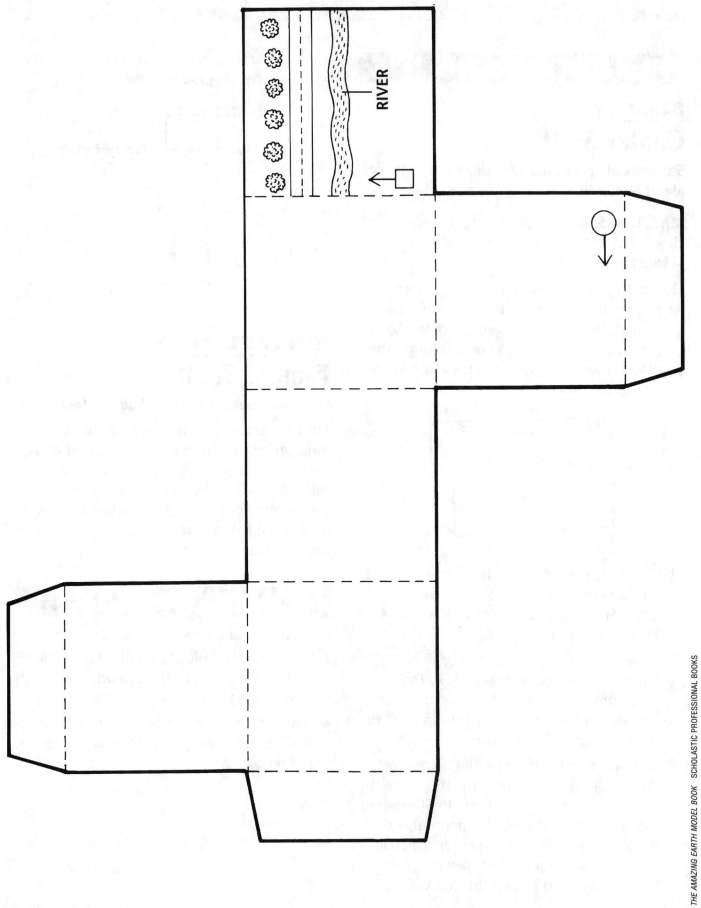

RIVER

*THE AMAZING EARTH MODEL BOOK*  SCHOLASTIC PROFESSIONAL BOOKS

FOCUS

WATERFALL

FOCUS

ROAD

# Earthquake Energy Waves

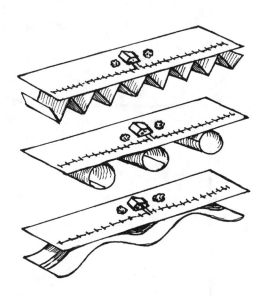

## Catch the Wave

These models demonstrate the three kinds of earthquake energy waves.

### SCIENCE CONCEPTS & OBJECTIVES

◗ Infer how energy waves released during an earthquake can make rocks vibrate

◗ Relate the energy released by earthquakes to damage to life and property

### VOCABULARY

**L-waves**  surface long earthquake energy waves

**P-waves**  primary earthquake energy waves

**S-waves**  secondary earthquake energy waves

## For Your Information

When rocks snap apart during an earthquake, they can release a tremendous amount of energy in a few seconds. This energy travels out in all directions from the earthquake's focus as vibrations or energy waves. There are three kinds of earthquake energy waves: primary waves (P-waves), secondary waves (S-waves), and surface long waves (L-waves). P-waves make rocks vibrate back and forth. They are the fastest of the earthquake energy waves. S-waves shake rocks from side to side. And L-waves can make Earth's surface near the epicenter move up and down. L-waves are the most destructive of the earthquake energy waves.

## TEACHING WITH THE MODEL

## Catch the Wave

1. Ask students: What happens to land during an earthquake? *(It can move, shift, rise, and/or crack open.)* What can happen to homes, schools, bridges, and highways? *(They can be damaged or even destroyed.)* What do you think causes destruction during an earthquake? *(the vibrations)*

2. Invite students to make the models (see page 107).

3. Set the P-waves piece on a desk and place the aerial house scene on top of it. Grasp the P-waves piece at both ends and push and pull it, in and out, accordion style.

# Making the Model

## Catch the Wave

**MATERIALS:** reproducible page 109 ◎ scissors ◎ tape ◎ plastic bag twist ties ◎ 3 markers ◎ crayons, markers, or colored pencils (optional)

1. Reproduce page 109.

2. Cut out all four pieces along the solid black outer lines. Color the house scene, if desired.

3. Fold the P-waves piece accordion style along the dashed lines, as shown. Crease well.

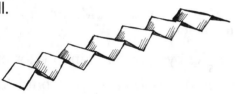

4. Tape a twist tie where indicated on the middle strip of the S-waves piece.

Curve the S-waves piece, as shown.

5. Cut the L-waves piece into three sections along the lines. Roll each section around a marker and tape, as shown.

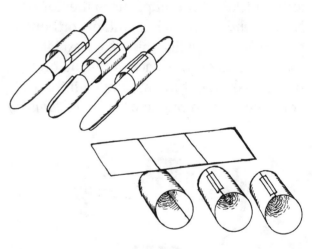

This mimics how P-waves given off during an earthquake cause rock to move back and forth.

4. Set the S-waves piece down and place the house scene on top of it. Rock the S-waves piece from side to side to mimic the effect of S-waves on the rocks they travel through.

5. Set the three markers, with the L-waves pieces wrapped around them, side by side. Place the house scene on top of the markers. Then roll the three markers. Challenge students to describe what happens. *(The scene moves up and down just like Earth's surface does when L-waves travel through rocks.)*

## EXTENSIONS

### HANDS-ON
## Making Waves

**Students further investigate the differences among P, S, and L earthquake energy waves.**

**MATERIALS:** Slinky™ toy ◎ rope ◎ plastic basin ◎ warm water ◎ large plastic lid ◎ dominoes

1. Stretch out the Slinky™ on a table. Ask a student to quickly push and pull on one of

the open ends. Ask: What do you see? *(The Slinky™ shrinks and grows accordion style.)* What kind of earthquake energy waves are like this? *(P-waves)*

2. Have two students hold the rope between them. Ask them to gently shake the rope from side to side so a wave snakes along it. Ask: What do you see? *(a wave)* What kind of earthquake energy waves are like this? *(S-waves)*

3. Fill the plastic basin with warm water and float the lid on it. Ask a student to put a hand into the water and move it back and forth quickly. What happens to the lid? *(It bobs up and down.)* What kind of earthquake energy waves are like this? *(L-waves)* Pile some dominoes in a stack on the lid and repeat. Ask: What might happen if the dominoes were a building? *(It would tumble.)*

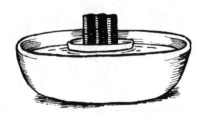

## COOPERATE AND CREATE
# Where Did They Go?

**Students investigate where earthquake energy waves go.**

Some earthquake energy waves travel deep inside Earth. Others just travel along Earth's surface. Divide students into groups and assign each either P-, S-, or L-waves. Challenge the groups to find out where their energy waves go and draw the path of their waves on the Inside Earth model (see page 11).

## RESEARCH IT

Related topics for research reports or projects:

➤ Report on the San Francisco earthquake of 1906 or 1989, or the 1964 Alaskan earthquake.

➤ How do people today try to prevent earthquake damage to their cities and towns?

➤ What are tsunamis?

## EARTHQUAKES RESOURCES

### BOOKS FOR STUDENTS

*Earthquakes* by Franklyn M. Branley (Crowell, 1990)

*Earthquakes* by Seymour Simon (Morrow, 1991)

*Mountains and Volcanoes* by Barbara Taylor (Kingfisher, 1993)

### BOOKS FOR TEACHERS

*Earthquakes and Geological Discovery* by Bruce A. Bolt (Scientific American Library, 1993)

*Earthquakes: Mind-Boggling Experiments You Can Turn Into Science Fair Projects* by Janice VanCleave (Wiley, 1993)

### OTHER RESOURCES

*The U.S. Geological Survey* offers informational booklets and activities related to earthquakes. For more information write: U.S. Geological Survey Information Services, P.O. Box 25286, Denver, CO 80225. Or call 800-HELP-MAP.

L-WAVES

L-WAVES

L-WAVES

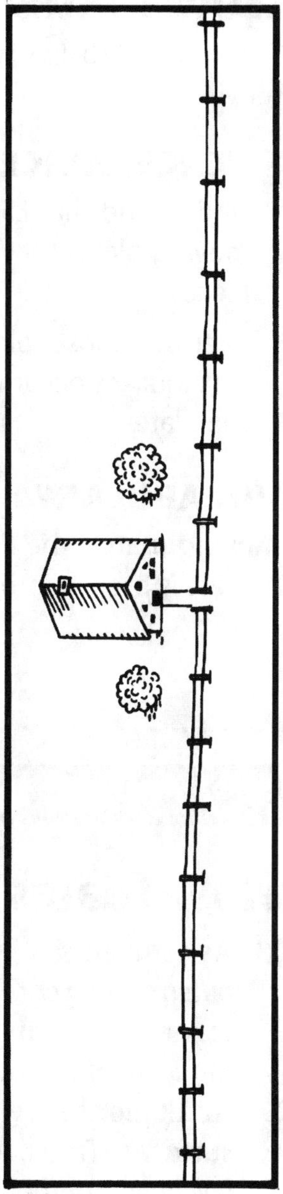

TAPE TWIST TIE HERE.

S-WAVES

P-WAVES

P-WAVES

# Plates on the Move

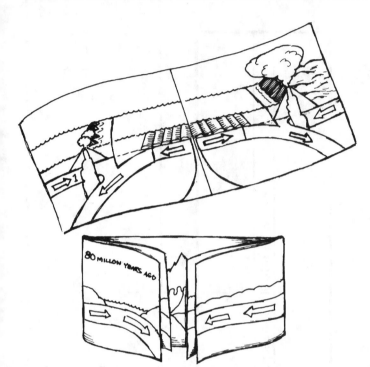

## How Plates Create

This model explains what happens as plates move.

### SCIENCE CONCEPTS & OBJECTIVES

- Understand that Earth's crust is broken into moving plates that fit together like puzzle pieces
- Infer that most volcanic eruptions and earthquakes occur where they do because of the plates

### VOCABULARY

**moving plates** the thick, rigid pieces Earth's crust is broken into

## For Your Information

Most scientists believe that Earth's crust is broken into about 20 pieces called *plates*. Each plate is the thickness of the crust and the rigid upper mantle. The plates move slowly, floating on the mushy, flowing mantle below them. Some of the plates move up to two inches (five centimeters) a year. That's about as fast as a fingernail grows.

The surface of some plates is mostly ocean, while that of others is made up of entire continents and parts of oceans. Where two plates meet, they can spread apart, come together, or slide past each other. These interactions between plates—and the intense pressure, friction, and crust melting they create—are responsible for much of our planet's volcanic and earthquake activity. They also build mountains and recycle Earth's crust.

## TEACHING WITH THE MODEL

## How Plates Create

1. Ask students: What is Earth's crust? *(the outermost layer of rock that surrounds Earth)* Is the crust a single solid piece? *(No, it's made up of 20 moving plates.)* How do you think giant moving plates change Earth's surface? *(They can create mountains, volcanoes, and earthquakes.)*

2. Invite students to make the model (see page 111).

3. Ask students to place the two rectangles they taped together in front of them. They should also have the nine lettered pieces and glue handy.

# Making the Model ✂

## How Plates Create

**MATERIALS:** reproducible pages 114–116 ○ scissors ○ tape or glue ○ crayons or markers (optional)

1. Photocopy pages 114–116.

2. Cut out the large rectangle on page 114 and set it to the left.

3. Cut out the large rectangle on page 115 and set it to the right.

4. Bring the two rectangles together, side by side, and tape together, as shown. The numbers about midway down each page should read 1 to 4 from left to right.

5. Cut out the nine pieces on page 116.

6. Color all the pieces, if desired.

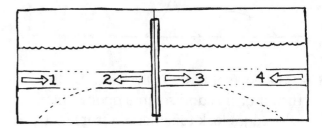

---

4. Explain that they are looking at parts of four plates. Each plate is numbered with arrows showing its direction of movement. Most of each plate's surface is ocean. Have students identify the four plates on their model and each one's direction of movement.

5. Ask students to look at the center of the model. There the edges of plates 2 and 3 are spreading apart. This opens giant cracks called *rifts* in the seafloor. Have students find the A on their model and then paste piece A on that outlined spot. It

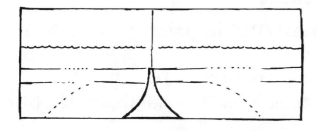

shows that hot magma rises and slowly oozes out of the rifts as lava. As the lava cools, it builds underwater mountains. Label piece A, MAGMA.

6. Paste pieces B and C in their places. Explain that as plates 2 and 3 move apart, they act like giant conveyor belts moving the mountains away from the cracks. More mountains form in their place. In this way, underwater mountain ranges called *ridges* build up. Label B and C, RIDGES.

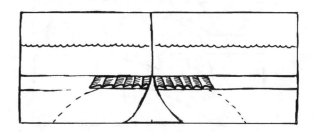

**7.** Focus attention on the edges of plates 1 and 2 that are moving toward each other. Where they meet, the edge of 2 bends and dives under 1. This forms a *trench*. Paste piece D in its place and label it TRENCH.

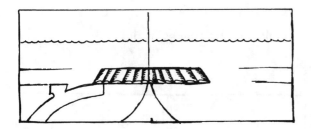

**8.** As the edge of plate 2 dives into Earth's crust, it grinds and scrapes against plate 1. If the edges lock together, pressure can build, causing an earthquake.

**9.** High heat inside the crust melts the edge of plate 2 into magma. Some of the magma may rise and break through the seafloor. Put piece E in its place and paste down the bottom half. Label it MAGMA.

**10.** Magma that erupts from the seafloor can build up a line of island volcanoes called a *volcanic arc*. Paste piece F in place; it fits behind piece E. (Students can paste the rest of piece E to piece F now.) Label piece F, VOLCANIC ARC. Point out that Japan, the Philippines, and the Aleutian Islands off Alaska are parts of volcanic arcs.

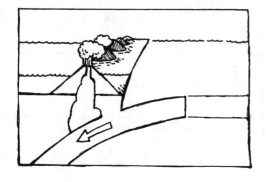

**11.** Focus attention on where plates 3 and 4 are moving toward each other. At the edge of 3 there is an ocean. At the edge of 4 there is a continent. Paste piece G in its place. Ask: What is it? *(a trench that forms when 3 dives under 4)* Label it TRENCH.

**12.** Put piece H in its place and paste down the bottom half. Ask: What is it? *(magma rising from the melting edge of 3)*

**13.** Paste piece I in its place, behind piece H. (Students can paste piece H to piece I now.) Ask: What is it? *(a line of volcanoes on land built from lava during eruptions)* Have students label piece I, VOLCANOES. Then point out that Mount St. Helens (see page 24) formed this way. Also, many earthquakes on land occur where the ocean edge of one plate dives under the continent edge of another.

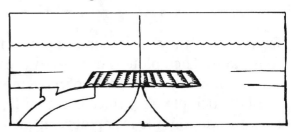

## EXTENSIONS

**HANDS-ON**

# Make a Mountain

**Students create mini-books showing how a mountain range forms when two plates collide.**

**MATERIALS:** reproducible page 117 ○ scissors ○ tape

**1.** Photocopy page 117.

**2.** Cut out the three pieces along the solid black outer lines.

3. Fold the ends of the 60 million years ago piece along the dashed lines. They should fold back, like tabs, with the printed side on the outside.

4. Place the 40 million years ago piece behind the 60 million years ago piece with the printed side facing in. Fit it inside the tabs and tape both ends, as shown.

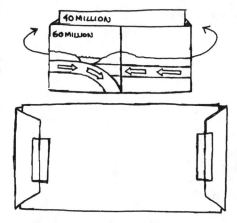

5. Cut through the vertical bold center line on the 60 million years ago piece.

6. Fold the ends of the 80 million years ago piece along the dashed lines. They should fold back, like tabs, with the printed side on the outside.

7. Place the 80 million years ago piece on top of the 60 million years ago piece and repeat steps 4 and 5.

8. Read Making the World's Tallest Mountain, below, to the class and have students follow along using their flap books. Then challenge them to write their own version on the flap book's blank areas.

## COOPERATE AND CREATE
# Name that Plate

**Students map Earth's plates.**

Research the names of Earth's moving plates as a class. Then assign student groups one of the plates. Have each group find out where the plate is, the direction in which the plate is moving, and what other plates it touches. Challenge the class to create a world map with the plates drawn on it, including the names of the plates and direction arrows.

## RESEARCH IT

Related topics for research reports or projects:

- Why is Iceland so affected by moving plates?

- What do scientists think causes the plates to move?

- What is the Ring of Fire?

# Making the World's Tallest Mountain

- It is 80 million years ago. The continents of India and Asia are on different moving plates with a sea separating them. The edge of India's plate bends and dives under Asia's plate.

- It is 60 million years ago. The sea has narrowed as the plates keep moving. The edge of India's plate keeps inching down the trench.

- It is 40 million years ago. The sea has disappeared as India finally reaches Asia—and rams into it! Sediments and the seafloor are squeezed between the colliding plates. The tremendous crash closes the trench, joins India to Asia, and raises part of the land to form the Himalaya mountains. The crash has created the world's tallest mountain—Everest.

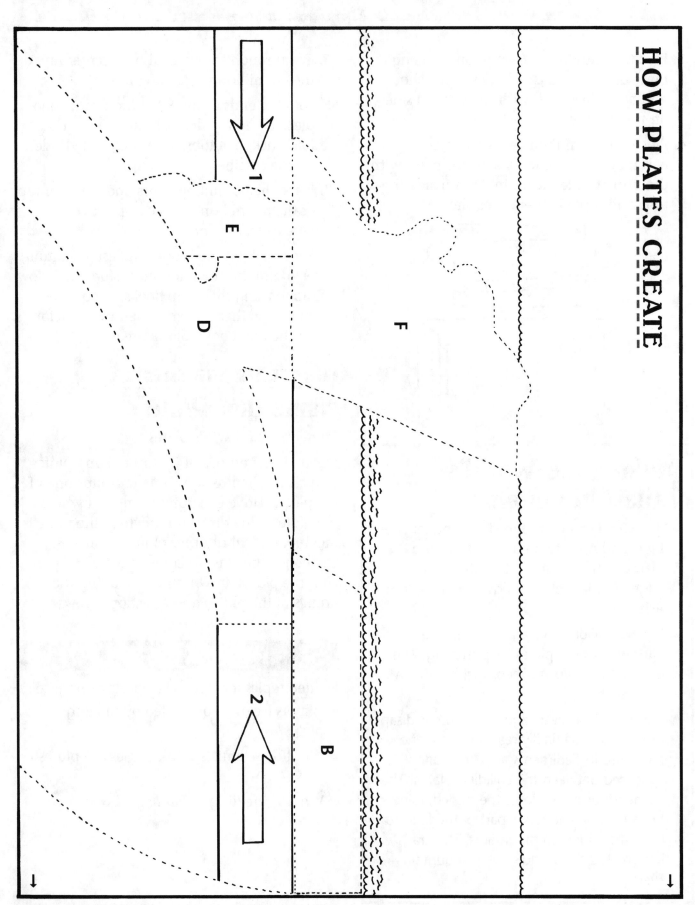

THE AMAZING EARTH MODEL BOOK   SCHOLASTIC PROFESSIONAL BOOKS

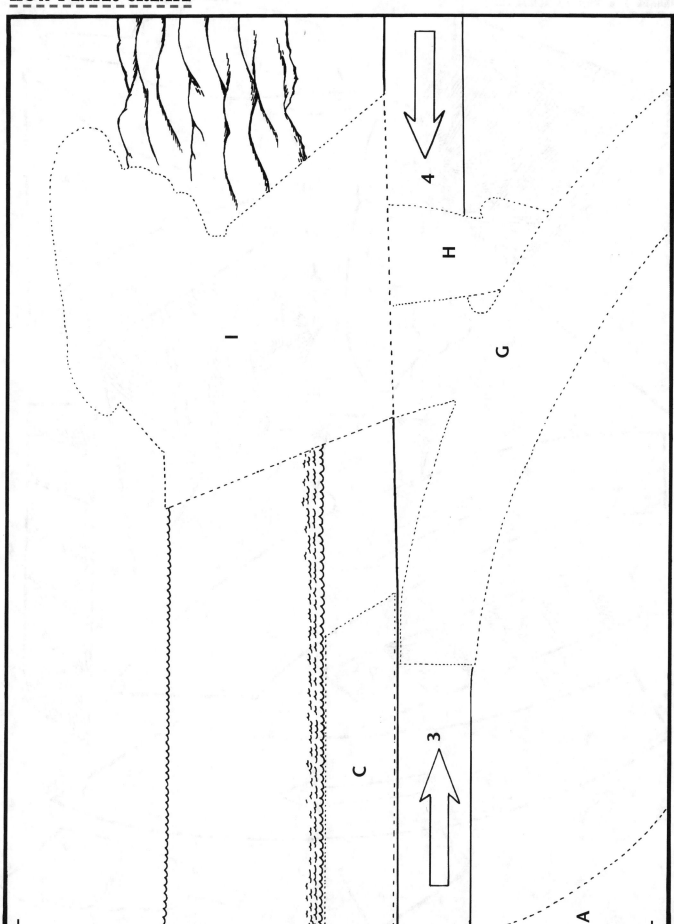

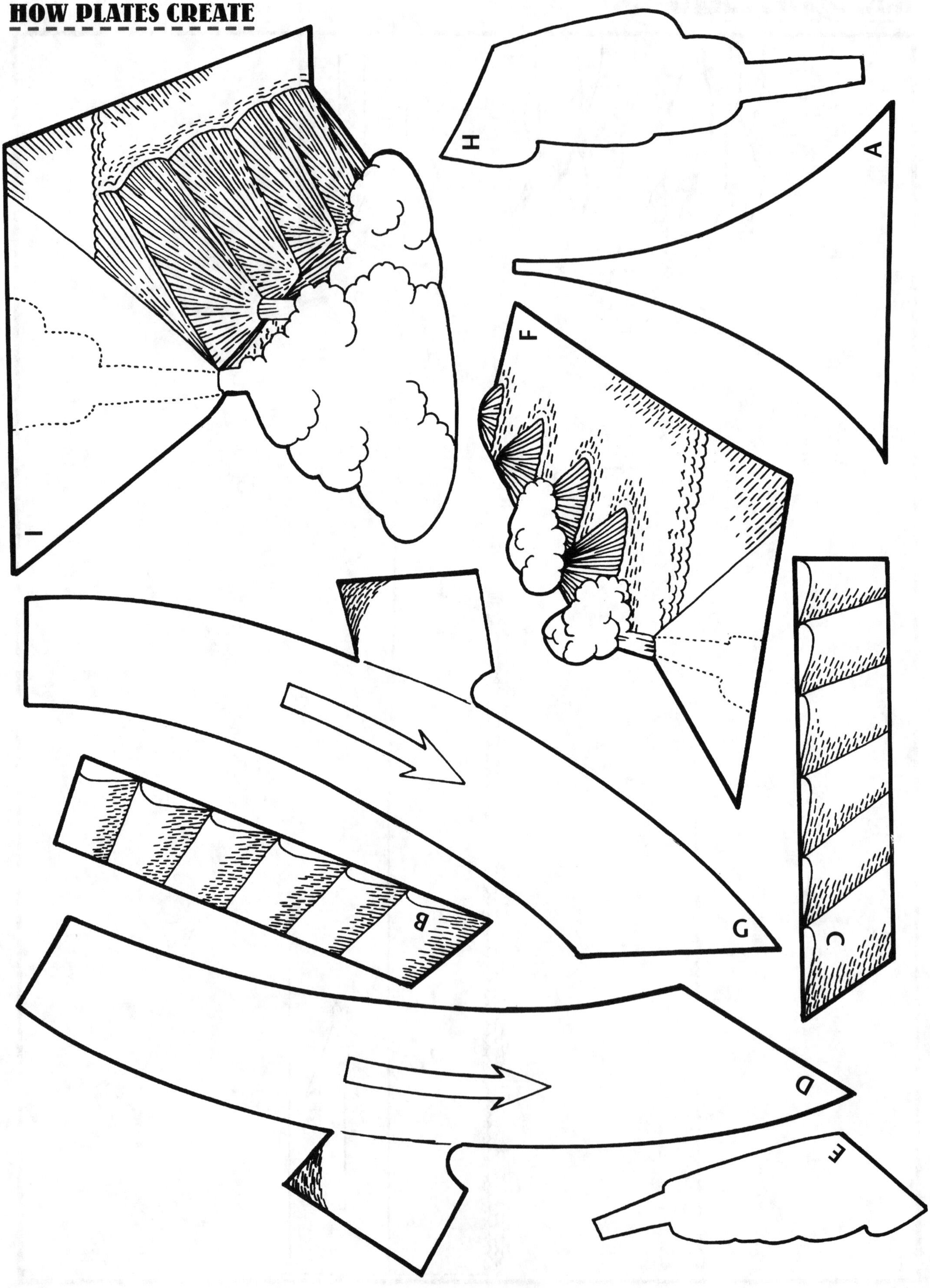
I
H
A
F
G
B
C
D
E

# MAKE A MOUNTAIN

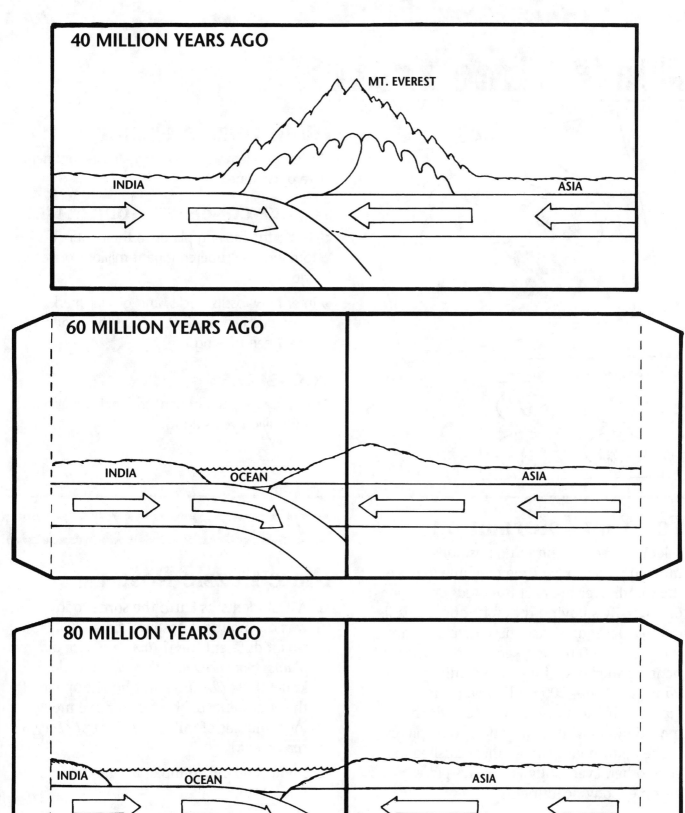

**40 MILLION YEARS AGO**

MT. EVEREST

INDIA          ASIA

**60 MILLION YEARS AGO**

INDIA     OCEAN          ASIA

**80 MILLION YEARS AGO**

INDIA     OCEAN          ASIA

# Plate Time Travel

Earth Today and Long ago

## Plate Puzzle Poster

This model demonstrates how all the continents were once joined.

### SCIENCE CONCEPTS & OBJECTIVES

◗ Relate the moving plates to the continents forming one supercontinent millions of years ago

◗ Infer how fossils, rocks, and glacier marks helped convince scientists that the continents have been moving

### VOCABULARY

**Pangaea** a supercontinent that existed about 240 million years ago

## For Your Information

Scientists use the changing positions of the moving plates like a time machine to trace their path over the past hundreds of millions of years. By studying rock formations, fossils, and glacier marks, scientists have evidence that about 240 million years ago all the continents formed one giant supercontinent called Pangaea. About 200 million years ago Pangaea broke apart into pieces, which moved along with their plates. Some pieces broke apart again while others crashed into each other. Eventually Pangaea's pieces became today's continents.

## TEACHING WITH THE MODEL

## Plate Puzzle Poster

1. Ask students: Is Earth the same today as it was during the dinosaurs' time? *(no)* How was it different then? *(hotter, wetter, different plants, more ocean, and so on)* How do we know that? *(fossils)* What has happened to the continents as the plates have moved for hundreds of millions of years? *(They've spread out.)*

2. Invite students to make the model (see page 119).

3. Have students set their Earth Today and Long Ago mini-posters where they can see and refer to them. Their plate puzzle pieces should be on a sheet of blue construction paper in front of them.

# Making the Model ✂

## Plate Puzzle Poster

**MATERIALS:** reproducible pages 122–124 ○ crayons, markers, or colored pencils ○ scissors ○ glue or tape ○ blue construction paper

1. Photocopy pages 122–124.

2. Cut out all nine pieces on pages 122–123. Color them, if desired.

3. Arrange the pieces on a sheet of blue construction paper, which represents the ocean.

4. Challenge students to create a map of today with the pieces, using the mini-poster's Today globe as a guide.

5. Explain that the hatched areas are where very old rock formations were found. The dashed areas represent places that have glacier marks on rocks. The animals and plants stand for specific fossils.

6. Challenge students to fit South America next to Africa so the very old rocks join, the glacier marks join, and the fossils link. These were clues that led the scientist Alfred Wegener to theorize that all the continents were once joined together. They formed the supercontinent, Pangaea (pan-GEE-uh), surrounded by one vast ocean called Panthalassa (pan-thuh-LOS-uh). (Pangaea means "all lands," Panthalassa means "all seas.")

7. Next, ask students to try to fit the rest of the pieces together to form a giant continent without looking at the mini-poster. (You might ask them to turn their mini-posters over.) After they've attempted it, allow them to check and correct using the 240 Million Years Ago globe on the mini-poster.

8. The continents were moving along with the plates below them before Pangaea formed and continue to spread today. Allow students to see two interim time periods by forming the 420 Million Years Ago and 65 Million Years Ago continent positions using the mini-poster's globes as guides. Ask: When did the dinosaurs become extinct? *(about 65 million years ago)* Are the continents still moving? *(yes)*

### HANDS-ON

# Moving Continents

**Students model how moving plates spread continents apart.**

**MATERIALS:** shoe box ● scissors ● sheet of paper ● tape ● 2 flat lumps of clay

1. Set the shoe box upside down with the long side in front of you. Cut out a rectangle on the box's front to make a wide "door." It needs to be big enough for your hand to fit into.

2. Cut the sheet of paper in half lengthwise to make two long strips. Tape the strips together at one end. Fold the strip in half at the taped midpoint.

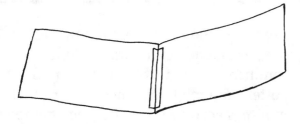

3. Using the width of the paper strip as a guide, cut a slot in the top of the box. It should run the width of the box. Make sure the paper strip fits easily into the slot.

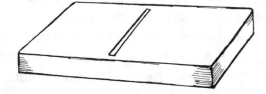

4. Put the paper strip into the slot, folded and taped end first. Fold back each side of the paper strip so it lays on top of the box.

5. Place a clay lump on the paper strip on each side, close to the slot.

6. The clay lumps represent continents, and the paper strip represents the plates. Put your hand inside the "door" and slowly push up the paper strip. Ask: What happens? *(As the ends of the paper move, the lumps of clay move away from each other.)* How is this like how continents spread? *(The paper is like the moving plates, spreading the continents apart.)* Ask: What do you think my hand represents? *(The force that moves the plates. Many scientists think that movement within the mushy part of Earth's mantle creates this force.)*

## COOPERATE AND CREATE
# Puzzling Future

**Students predict what the world of the future will look like.**

By studying how plates move, scientists not only go back in time but also can look into the future. They can predict how the continents will move based on current plate movement. Challenge student groups to move the map pieces into positions they predict the continents will reach 50, 100, and 250 million years from now. Have them sketch each time interval and label it. Then invite the groups to find out who agrees with them! Students can research what scientists are predicting and why. How close did they come?

## RESEARCH IT

Related topics for research reports or projects:

➧ Report on the scientist Alfred Wegener.

➧ How do the moving plates fit into the rock cycle (see page 55) and help explain it?

## MOVING PLATES RESOURCES

### BOOKS FOR STUDENTS

*Our Patchwork Planet: The Story of Plate Tectonics* by Helen Roney Sattler (Lothrop, Lee & Shepard, 1995)

### BOOKS FOR TEACHERS

*Moving Continents: Our Changing Earth* by Thomas G. Aylesworth (Enslow, 1990)

*Plate Tectonics: Earth's Shifting Crust* by Sean M. Grady (Lucent Books, 1991)

*Shaping the Earth: Tectonics of Continents and Oceans* by Eldridge M. Moores (W. H. Freeman, 1990)

*Voyages of Discovery: Our Changing Planet* by Editions Gallimard Jeunesse (Scholastic, 1995)

AFRICA &
ARABIAN
PENINSULA

GREENLAND

SOUTH
AMERICA

INDIA

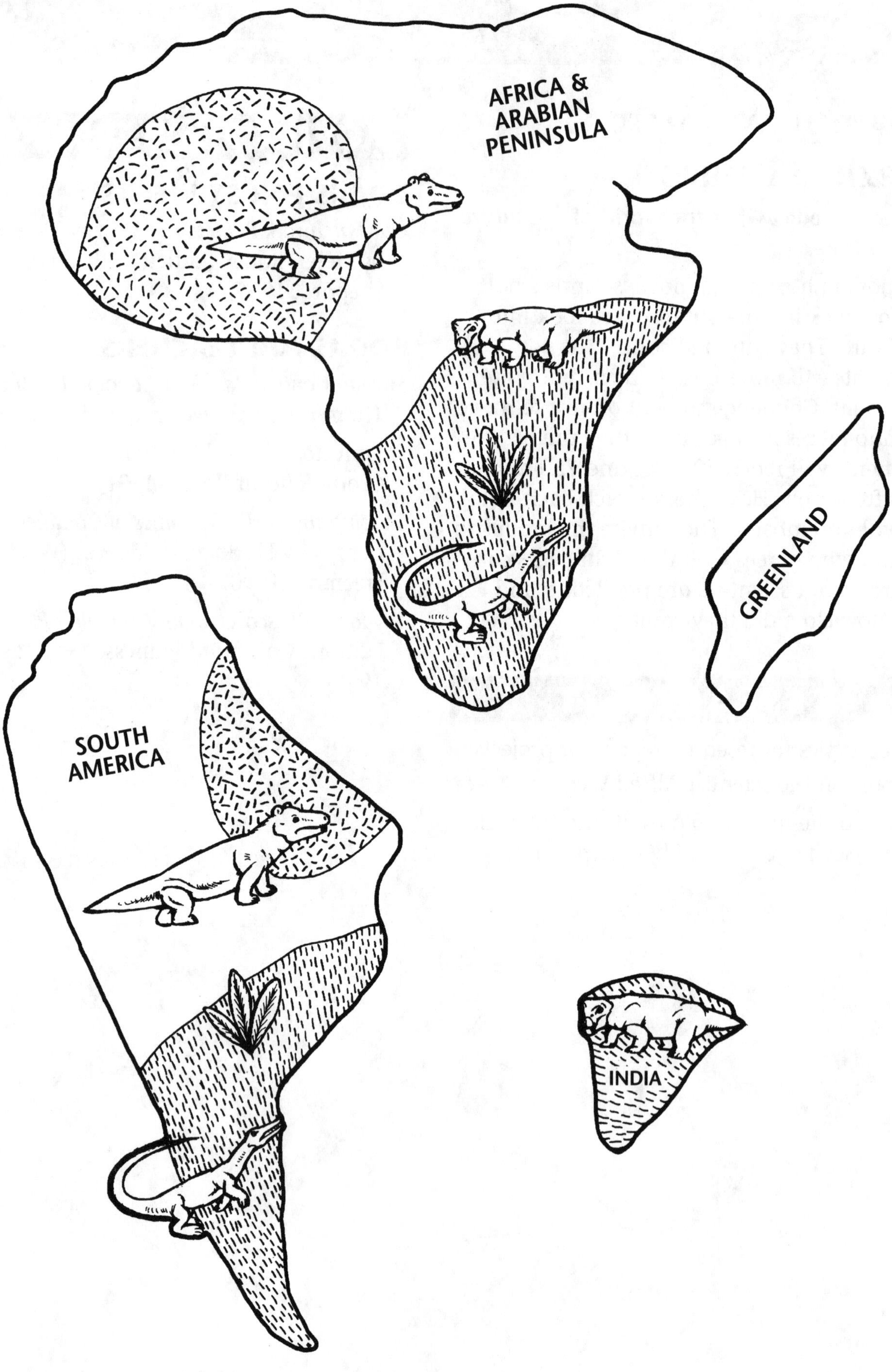

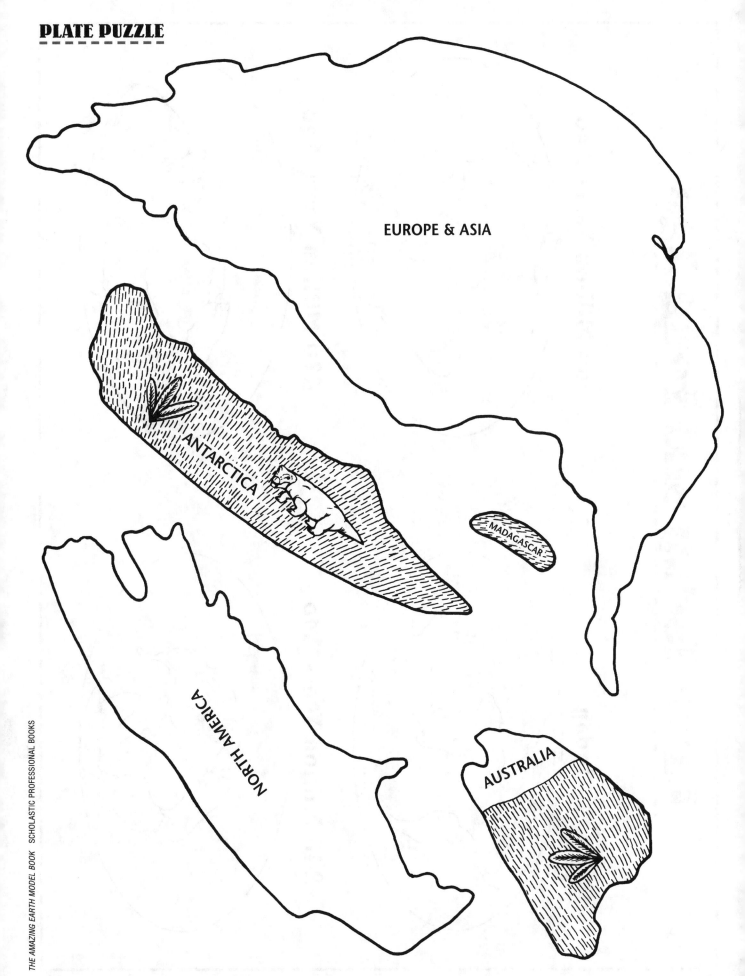

EUROPE & ASIA

ANTARCTICA

MADAGASCAR

NORTH AMERICA

AUSTRALIA

# Earth Today and Long Ago

## 65 Million Years Ago

## 420 Million Years Ago

## Today

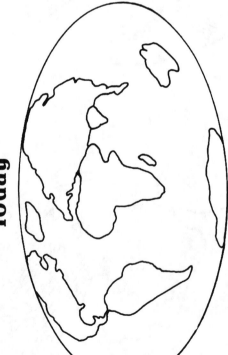

## 240 Million Years Ago

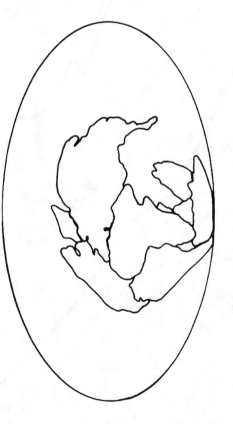

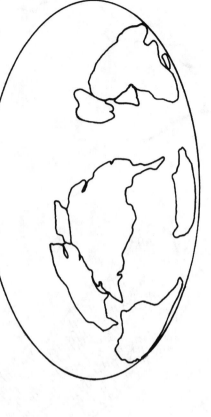

THE AMAZING EARTH MODEL BOOK   SCHOLASTIC PROFESSIONAL BOOKS

# RESOURCES

## VOLCANOES

### BOOKS FOR STUDENTS

*Mountains and Volcanoes* by Barbara Taylor (Kingfisher, 1993)

*Volcano: The Eruption and Healing of Mount St. Helens* by Patricia Lauber (Bradbury Press, 1986)

*Volcanoes* by Jacqueline Dineen (Gloucester Press, 1991)

### BOOKS FOR TEACHERS

*Fire on the Mountain: The Nature of Volcanoes* by Dorian Weisel (Chronicle Books, 1994)

*Volcanoes: Mind-Boggling Experiments You Can Turn Into Science Fair Projects* by Janice VanCleave (Wiley, 1994)

*Volcanoes* by Gregory Vogt (Franklin Watts, 1993)

### OTHER RESOURCES

*Scholastic's The Magic School Bus Explores Inside the Earth* Windows CD-ROM (Microsoft Home, 1996)

*Volcanoes: Life on the Edge* Mac/Windows CD-ROM (Corbis, 1995)

*What's the Earth Made Of?* Video (National Geographic Educational Technology, 1995)

## ROCKS & FOSSILS

### BOOKS FOR STUDENTS

*Eyewitness Explorers: Rocks and Minerals* by Steve Parker (Dorling Kindersley, 1993)

*One Small Square: Swamp* by Donald M. Silver and Patricia J. Wynne (McGraw-Hill, 1997)

*Rocks* by Terry Jennings (Garrett, 1991)

*Rocks & Minerals at Your Fingertips* by Judy Nayer (McClanahan, 1995)

### BOOKS FOR TEACHERS

*Eyewitness Books: Rocks & Minerals* by R. F. Symes (Knopf, 1988)

*Rocks & Fossils* by Ray Oliver (Random House, 1993)

*Rocks and Minerals: Mind-Boggling Experiments You Can Turn Into Science Fair Projects* by Janice VanCleave (Wiley, 1996)

### OTHER RESOURCES

*Geology: Rocks and Minerals* Mac/Windows CD-ROM (National Geographic Educational Technology, 1994)

*Message in a Fossil* Mac/PC CD-ROM (Steck-Vaughn, 1996)

# WEATHERING

## BOOKS FOR STUDENTS

*Caves and Caverns* by Gail Gibbons (Harcourt Brace, 1993)

*One Small Square: Backyard* and *Cave* by Donald M. Silver and Patricia J. Wynne (McGraw-Hill, 1997)

*Soil* by Karen Bryant-Mole (Raintree Steck-Vaughn, 1996)

*Underground Life* by Allan Roberts (Children's Press, 1983)

## BOOKS FOR TEACHERS

*Chiseling the Earth: How Erosion Shapes the Land* by R. V. Fodor (Enslow, 1983)

*Earth: The Ever Changing Planet* by Donald M. Silver (Random House, 1989)

*Earth Science Activities for Grades 2–8* by Marvin N. Tolman and James O. Morton (Prentice Hall, 1986)

## OTHER RESOURCES

*Ask-a-geologist* Geologists at the U.S. Geological Survey are available on-line to answer students' earth science questions (E-mail: usgs.gov).

*Geology: Weathering and Erosion* Mac/Windows CD-ROM (National Geographic Educational Technology, 1994)

*The National Speleological Society* 2813 Cave Avenue, Huntsville, AL 35810-4431 (E-mail: http://www.caves.org/~nss). Write or E-mail this organization to find out about caves near you.

*One Small Square: Backyard* Mac/Windows CD-ROM (Virgin Sound and Vision, 1995)

# WATER & EROSION

## BOOKS FOR STUDENTS

*Icebergs and Glaciers* by Seymour Simon (Morrow, 1987)

*Soil Erosion and Pollution* by Darlene R. Stille (Children's Press, 1990)

*Water Up, Water Down: The Hydrologic Cycle* by Sally M. Walker (Carolrhoda Books, 1992)

## BOOKS FOR TEACHERS

*Earth Science for Every Kid* by Janice VanCleave (Wiley, 1991)

*Great Rivers of the World* (National Geographic Society, 1984)

*Tapping Earth's Heat* by Patricia Lauber (Garrard, 1978)

## OTHER RESOURCES

*Explore Yellowstone* Mac/Windows CD-ROM (MECC/The Learning Co., 1996)

## EARTHQUAKES

### BOOKS FOR STUDENTS

*Earthquakes* by Franklyn M. Branley (Crowell, 1990)

*Earthquakes* by Seymour Simon (Morrow, 1991)

*Mountains and Volcanoes* by Barbara Taylor (Kingfisher, 1993)

### BOOKS FOR TEACHERS

*Earthquakes and Geological Discovery* by Bruce A. Bolt (Scientific American Library, 1993)

*Earthquakes: Mind-Boggling Experiments You Can Turn Into Science Fair Projects* by Janice VanCleave (Wiley, 1993)

### OTHER RESOURCES

*The U.S. Geological Survey* offers informational booklets and activities related to earthquakes. For more information write: U.S. Geological Survey Information Services, P.O. Box 25286, Denver, CO 80225. Or call 800-HELP-MAP.

## MOVING PLATES

### BOOKS FOR STUDENTS

*Our Patchwork Planet: The Story of Plate Tectonics* by Helen Roney Sattler (Lothrop, Lee & Shepard, 1995)

### BOOKS FOR TEACHERS

*Moving Continents: Our Changing Earth* by Thomas G. Aylesworth (Enslow, 1990)

*Plate Tectonics: Earth's Shifting Crust* by Sean M. Grady (Lucent Books, 1991)

*Shaping the Earth: Tectonics of Continents and Oceans* by Eldridge M. Moores (W. H. Freeman, 1990)

*Voyages of Discovery: Our Changing Planet* by Editions Gallimard Jeunesse (Scholastic, 1995)

# NOTES